W9-CFN-394

Janet Kauffman's

OBSCENE
GESTURES
FOR
WOMEN

"This collection of short stories displays a highly refined technique. The angers that animate its characters and events escape like controlled explosions.... These stories are really tales, with elements of mythic hyper-reality and metamorphoses.... Kauffman is finely tuned to the observation of details, with an especially keen ear for the pitch and melodies of her characters' ways of speaking."

—*Chicago Tribune*

"Janet Kauffman's short stories pose overtly feminist questions in a thoroughly undogmatic way. The opening story, a surrealistic fantasy, sets the scene: A man accidentally comes upon a flock of woman-birds in a field.... The voices in the stories that follow could be the individuals in this exotic flock."

—*Los Angeles Times*

"Fine...lovely, poetic stories about spiritually triumphant characters who move with the world, not against it."

—*Detroit Free Press*

"Her stories...set us down. Lock us up in themselves. Let us think. Eyes open. Geraniums hum. Craniums hum. Hearts hum. Kauffman doesn't abandon her poet's precision, her love of details and their teasing absence, or her lyricism on the slightly broader canvas of the short story. Nor does she lose her sense of place. The beauty of her women lies most clearly in their strength and their gentle courage, and in the language that creates them. These fifteen stories, which confirm Kauffman's reputation as an important voice, are not loud or flashy. But I'd be willing to lock myself up for another hour or so, and see what else starts humming...."

—*Houston Chronicle*

"Kauffman can crystallize a personality with lovely clarity."

—*People*

"Throughout her work, Kauffman has shown a deep concern for the balance between autonomy and community, especially for women....Kauffman's stories are not hearty or sentimental. [They] make room for God's small acts of rejuvenation....There are enough secrets revealed to make several readings a pleasure."

—*Village Voice*

"The women in *Obscene Gestures for Women* are independent, spirited, intelligent and hard-edged....Their stories are designed to probe the differences between men and women. Kauffman's politics are never overstated, and [she has a] talent for the language of love and sexuality....Writing doesn't get any better than that."

—*Kansas City Star*

OBSCENE
GESTURES
FOR
WOMEN

ALSO BY JANET KAUFFMAN

The Weather Book

Places in the World a Woman Could Walk

Collaborators

Where the World Is

JANET KAUFFMAN

STORIES

OBSCENE GESTURES FOR WOMEN

VINTAGE CONTEMPORARIES
VINTAGE BOOKS
A DIVISION OF RANDOM HOUSE, INC.
NEW YORK

FIRST VINTAGE CONTEMPORARIES EDITION, NOVEMBER 1990

Copyright © 1984, 1986, 1987, 1988, 1989 by Janet Kauffman

All rights reserved under International and Pan-American
Copyright Conventions. Published in the United States by
Vintage Books, a division of Random House, Inc., New York,
and simultaneously in Canada by Random House of Canada
Limited, Toronto. Originally published in hardcover by Alfred
A. Knopf, Inc., in 1989.

Library of Congress Cataloging-in-Publication Data
Kauffman, Janet.
    Obscene gestures for women : stories / Janet Kauffman.—1st
    Vintage contemporaries ed.
        p.   cm.
    ISBN 0-679-73055-9
    I. Title.
    [PS3561.A82027   1990]
    813′.54—dc20   90-50165
                        CIP

Some of these stories were originally published in *Forehead*,
The Paris Review, The PEN Syndicated Fiction Project, and *The
Quarterly*. "News" was originally published in *The Missouri
Review*; "Machinery," "How Sunlight Figures In," and "Where
I'd Quit" were originally published in *The New Yorker*; and
"Women over Bay City" was originally published in *Sulfur*.

Manufactured in the United States of America
10 9 8 7 6 5 4 3 2 1

THIS BOOK IS FOR JEFF

AND FOR MELINDA

AND FOR BILL AND ANN

CONTENTS

CONTENTS

OBSCENE
GESTURES
FOR
WOMEN

WOMEN
OVER
BAY CITY

And then they came down, all of the women, and settled in the field. Only the long necks showed above stubble.

He thought, what of it? What difference does it make if I move or don't move? He didn't move.

And more of them, beyond what he had imagined, appeared over the highway. At first they were birds. But then they were not birds. Their arms arched, slung away from the body, pulled back. They were synchronous as a flock.

Lowering out of the sky, they turned first into the wind, and then circled, lower, around, and once more into the wind. Their hair blew out across their shoulders, or lifted in coarse strands. They had thin, wild bodies. He noticed the tendons pull through their necks, and he noticed the nacreous sheen of their knees, the caps of bone. They had breasts like drawings of breasts, half circles on brown paper.

As they approached and turned themselves into the field, arms lowering more, stiffening, he registered the disturbance they made in the air. The push of wind. Their legs angled forward, the thighs taut. Then the feet turned up, and he understood the aerodynamic precision of their landing. He breathed sharply through his nose, to catch a scent.

They came in by the thousands.

What could there be in the field but stubble? Remnants. After the harvest had taken place, whenever that was, the broken-up stalks had bleached out and shattered. The leaves were not leaves but streamers of crepe, blown around, brittle.

If they came here for food, that was something new for the books. He couldn't think what it would be.

Besides, having landed, they stood absolutely still, their bodies obscured except for the long necks, the small heads, dark with the sun behind them, like new plants, or dried pods.

No one would notice, happening by at this moment. He knew it was chance—that he'd seen anything.

The women didn't feed. They didn't move.

After a while, with the sun continuing, an idea poured through his mind, over his shoulders. He wrapped himself in it.

He wondered how long a man could live, without moving a muscle.

I have seen women pull a lot of stunts, he thought. But nothing like this. I believe I'm a lucky man.

And he breathed so slowly, air moved in its ordinary way around his face, undisturbed. He had already sworn to himself: I'll stay. Something will happen. One of them, sooner or later, will take off. Or speak.

MACHINERY

I don't have a heart of steel.

I try to explain this to my son, Harry, who is sixteen and in trouble. "Your life is a small thing," I tell him. "Don't exaggerate. Don't blow it up."

But advice is nothing. What can it prove? My husband, Claude, agrees, and he says to me, "Write him a song. Then he'll listen."

But what Harry needs to hear is noise. Forget the words. Harry should work awhile with machinery, with a machine that is multipurpose, oversize, with a two-hundred-page manual. If he knew one machine, knew it backwards and forwards, he'd at least know more than himself.

When we work in the barn, spray-painting equipment, Harry props the radio on a galvanized bin. He says he can hear it above the compressor. He sings along, and I can hear him: "I'm traveling," the words go, "into your arms." Walking back from the barn, I point to the baler and tell him, "That's where you ought to travel. Or into a foreign country."

"I'm into music," he says.

I think he should study something less human, something that doesn't breathe, and when I say so, that's when he says, "You have a heart of steel."

I have learned this much about machinery: it has no life of its own. If you track it back to its origins, and there's no reason you shouldn't, machinery is rock. And the more you ride it or work at it—the more bolts and valves and bearings you replace— the more the machinery loses momentum, and stills itself, and reduces itself to the elements.

Soon, when you drive around town and see the factories, especially in the summer, with their huge doors open for ventilation, and you look inside at the screw machines, what you see there is rock, in shapes not so different from what you would see in the deserts of Utah. And outside, in the fields, machinery presents itself, even painted John Deere green, as so many scraps of landscape.

I remind Harry: cars go in any direction. Airplanes, carved from rock and catapulted, fly easily city to city. Think of the people pushing aside the stone doors, moving in and out.

Think of a couple of people, I say to Harry, think of anybody—say, Pat Ravenel and me—riding an ordinary John Deere combine, Model 3300, harvesting two rows of corn at a time. I say to Harry: this is the modern world, mechanized. Give yourself ten years or so driving machinery before you draw conclusions.

But Harry is interested in songs, those words in the air, all about the heart, and hearts of steel.

It is possible to farm thirty-five acres with small machinery, and we do. For the combining, though, I hire Pat. From what I've seen, he understands the natural heritage of machinery. When he starts up the 3300, he climbs back out of the cab and stands on the ground, listening, the way you listen at the edge of the woods to an unseen stream, which is water running over rock, the sound you expect.

Pat owns this combine. And because, like everybody else, he also holds a job in town, farm work is always evening work. He does custom combining, and for three nights every November, he harvests the corn in our fields—two small fields, with 120 bushel corn, a good yield on poor ground, which we sell at low prices.

It's the same every year. I ride with him in the cab as we run the machine over the rows, for the same reason, I suppose, that some people ride the machinery in a park, the Ferris wheel, up and over, around the hub, the same thing, watching the ground move.

Machines open up the world and give you a ride through your own territory. You ride a rock; it's another point of view.

I've tried to talk about this with Harry. He says he knows the 3300 does a lot of things at once. It does. The machine cuts the corn, pulls the stalks inside, runs the ears between rollers to shell them, joggles it all on a sieve, then augers the kernels into its bin, and fans out the husks and debris, like exhaust. The machine—it's a cave—fills up with sound. I say, "Take a ride. See for yourself." But Harry wants to carry along his headphones, his tapes, and I say, "No, you can't."

To talk in the cab, Pat and I have to shout. We shout about our kids. We shout about the weather. We yell back and forth about the deer, whose disk eyes look back, each time we turn at the end of a row. It's the only time all year that we talk.

I don't like to miss these rides. When I hear the machine, I stop what I'm doing in the house and head outside.

This year, November 5th, when Pat drives the combine down the road, it's already dark. He shifts out of road gear, I hear that, and heads back the lane. I leave the supper table and grab a coat. Claude and Harry expect all this, and they wave good-bye. Claude throws a kiss. "See you later," he says. Harry's lips go shut, humming.

Outside, the wind hits my back. I walk fast on the path, but the combine travels faster than walking speed, a quarter mile ahead, and I won't catch up until it stops.

Out of range of the yard light, there is the pitch black of the field, flat as a wall, and the ground hits hard against the soles of my boots. I try running, slow and easy, not looking down, and that works fine. The house pulls back into small squares of light. There's a wild, blind rattling of dry stalks—the alfalfa stems under my feet where I don't look, and the snap of leaves in the cornfield, where I can't see.

Up ahead, the lights of the combine aim toward the farthest cornfield. The engine noise, a great droning, fills the space overhead; the noise rises and closes over, like sky.

At the end of the lane, what I come upon is a small scene, spotlighted. The combine is idling, and Pat's on his back under the machine, greasing the chains. I can see his feet in the light around the tires.

When he stands up, he yells something about the wind. He

sets the grease gun in a toolbox, and he takes off his cap. The world roars, and the leaves of the cornstalks, blond in the headlights, all of them point like streamers, south.

Pat climbs into the cab of the combine, and I climb next. We swing the steel steps up, hook them out of the way of stalks, and shut the door. The noise shifts inside. Wind blasts through a steel ventilating grid behind us, and Pat props a square of cardboard there, to block the cold. He shifts the combine into gear, and the machine moves around, slow as an airliner on its minuscule wheels, taxiing, with the same push, the enormous sigh, of hydraulic cylinders, powering itself this way and that way, angling into the first rows.

"I didn't see you!" Pat shouts.

"It doesn't matter!" I shout back.

As the combine hits the first stalks, Pat leans forward, engages the chains, and then we proceed, the noise and vibration shaking the seat.

"Wild!" Pat yells in my ear. He smells like mint, and soap. He's washed his neck.

We ride without talking up a slope, very gradual, where the oncoming stalks are as tall as the windshield. We look right at them. After a while, Pat pulls in a sharp breath, ready to talk.

"Keep your fingers crossed. There's two new bearings! Hear how smooth?"

"Smooth!" I yell back.

"Hey! On the way from Toledo," he shouts, "I thought I saw a UFO! Pulled over, couldn't believe it!"

"What?"

"A UFO! There were lights! These lights over a field. And I pulled onto the shoulder!"

"What was it?" I shout.

"It went slow! And then I knew what it was. This! Out in

the field. This!" he shouts, and points at us. "Just these lights!"

He takes another deep breath. He loosens the zipper at the top of his coveralls, and shakes his head. He doesn't look at me to talk—he watches the rows for rocks. This field is a glacial dump, with scattered, head-sized rocks; and so when he takes a breath to talk, I have to lean toward him, my ear near his mouth.

"People say they've seen UFOs! I don't know!"

"That happened with me," I shout. "Only it was an ambulance out there! Red lights!"

He turns his head—a glance up from the corn rows. "Whitey seen one!"

"What?"

"I don't know! He came in sunburned and says he seen a UFO hanging on a pine tree. I said, 'Whitey, I don't need it!' " Pat laughs. "But Whitey sees his grandma's ghost! She walks in his kitchen in her high heels. Clicks her damn high heels! That's how he knows!" Pat shouts.

We turn at the end of the row, and are silent riding back. The hopper fills with corn behind us, ticking against the steel sides, like sleet.

Without talk, the noise of the machinery takes over. It fills my ears, and it moves around inside my mouth, shaking my teeth. The stalks continue their slump, one after another, into the machine, and there's so much to see, looking ahead: the southward veering of the tassels; a flailing of long leaves, bleached out, ribbed like crepe paper.

On the return row, Pat shouts, "How's your arm?" He asks each year, and it's been three years since the surgery.

"Fine!" I tap my fingertips on the windshield. "I can feel the cold. How's *your* arm?" His accident was long ago.

"Great!" he says, and he waves his right arm, exercises the

elbow up and down. "I nearly lost it!" he shouts. "But this one doctor says let's wait. He was my buddy! Don't let yourself in a hospital if you can help it!"

"I won't!"

"Nobody gives you good-night kisses! You can live there, but it's no life. They treated me okay! I was in three months."

"Nobody gave you good-night kisses?" I laugh, and the laugh takes visible shape in the cold, and then I duck my head, to hear what he says.

"No! Anybody give *you* good-night kisses?"

"None!"

"See!" he shouts. He waves his arm at the field again. He looks back to check the corn in the bin, and it's nearly full.

"Harry got caught shoplifting again!" I shout.

"What!"

"A couple of records! He's doing community service. Two months!"

"What'd he take? Not Mozart!" he shouts.

"No!"

"Here's music," he says, and he pounds the steering wheel. He sings a loud note. "Opera's on tomorrow! I'll bring the radio!" He takes a breath. "Harry's a good boy!"

"He steals!"

"Harry's a good kid!"

At the end of the row, we pull up to a gravity wagon parked on the lane and empty out the bin. Pat switches a spotlight onto the chute, where the corn dumps out, in a stream like gold, very fluid, in the light.

I'm not sure what the accident was that tore up Pat's arm. Yelling back and forth, it's hard to catch the details, even over a period of years. I know he wrecked his truck. I know he doesn't blame anybody, not even himself. He's also told me, and these

are his words, "Opera is the call of the wild." As for the rest,
I don't know who Whitey is. Or his grandmother. It's work,
this talk.

I notice it every year. Sometimes we have so much to say to
each other. And sometimes we have nothing.

"Margaret's moved to Fennville!" Pat says, as we pull back
into the field. Margaret is his daughter. He describes her
house—how she's fixing it up, building a stairwell. She works
in a hospital, and we talk more about hospitals, the new machinery there, but half of what we say gets lost.

Finally we quit shouting and just ride, sometimes pointing
at the leaves, if the wind picks up, or pointing at the eyes of
the deer.

After an hour or so, Pat motions toward the lane, and I see
two lights, car lights, turning our way. The car moves slowly;
the lights hover. The lane is rough, and whoever is driving takes
it easy, very careful. It could be Claude, or Pat's wife, with
coffee. But it's late. It has to be Harry, with no license, out for
a drive. He's got the radio on, I know it; he's taking his time.
The car moves so slowly a person could walk alongside.

I don't know who Pat thinks is in the car. He stares ahead,
watching the ground. And that's what I do, too. The machine,
in low gear, crashes into the stalks, and it'll be a while until we
reach the end of the row.

OBSCENE GESTURES FOR WOMEN

Marimba had beautiful teeth. They were not especially good teeth, or strong, but they were well honed—small, white as the white keys on a piano, and level as the rosewood keys, come to think of it, on a marimba.

When she smiled, her front teeth rested on her lower lip, and she felt the angle, the beveling, identical tooth to tooth.

They were not her original teeth, not exactly, although they were hers, and not fake. They were ground-down teeth. Worn to a surface sameness and sheen, like rocks set down at a glacier's mouth. Fresh. So smooth. An astonishingly polished by-product of a fiercely tormented process.

In the end, Marimba thought of it as nature at work.

.   .   .

Marimba ground her teeth at night. And because she slept through that labor—and for years knew nothing of it—she for a long time woke up serene, with confidence in human achievement. She never considered why she held out hope for humanity, except that a livable life, with some effort, seemed possible: livable life on a livable planet. Some passion. Some ease. The knowledge of terror, but no terror. Political action. Research. Few psychiatrists. No war. Bread and butter and Parmesan. Salad greens. Death when it came, as it came.

She tried not to simplify, but there it was.

Her jaw grew powerful; her face toned with the exercise. And still, in her ignorance, she thought when she looked in the mirror: this is how a woman's face matures. She was pleased to see some of the sweetness disappear.

It was her mother who said, one morning on a summer visit: "Marimba. My God, you grind your teeth. It's a factory sound. It sounded like machinery in there. Rocks. Quarries. It was a terrible racket. You ought to see somebody."

And the next morning, barging into the bathroom while Marimba was brushing her teeth: "Honey, what's wrong? You're lucky you have any teeth left." Her mother bared her own teeth, a wild face in the mirror, and tapped her cockeyed front tooth. "Why don't you make an appointment to see somebody? Man-o-day, how can what's-his-name sleep with that racket?"

"His name is Michael."

"My God, how can the man sleep with that racket?"

A few things began to come back to Marimba then. Her elaborate cartoon dreams, for instance, where in the end, it came as no surprise—not to the compassionate trees, not to the zoo animals on the loose in living color, not to the hero-beast him- or herself—when the ordinary and unremarkable teeth of the hero-creature, in consequence of nothing, cracked, grew larger somehow with fracture lines, and crumbled apart, through many frames, to the ground. It happened in precise, slow motion. Fine line drawings webbed across the surface of the teeth, and with a machine noise—engine noise, earthquake noise—that clamped everybody else's jaws flat shut, the open-mouthed hero-animal's teeth cracked into chip-sized pieces and fell very thoroughly apart.

And then the jaw jammed and ground, and the tooth pieces crushed to particles, some to sand.

As at the end of all dreams, the dreamer vacuums the imagery and spirit of the dream into the waking mind, and Marimba woke up with her tongue scanning her teeth, thinking: Lord! Cataclysmic. The cartoon sense of order. Complete, causeless. It interested her that the impossible, the incredible, could exist in cartoon, simply because they could be conceived, and drawn.

She rubbed her jaw and praised the power of the mind, for dreaming up and producing such shows. She understood dreams as mindful dramas. She always gave them plenty of thought.

In fact, through the years, Marimba developed complex theories concerning cartoon dreams. Sometimes, in conversations at picnics, for example, she let those theories out, as theories of art: they sounded pretty good. But the same ideas, applied to the livable world, led to some distress, and she knew it. The incredible, the horrific, *could* be conceived, and drawn.

And carried out.

But there she was. In the forest preserve. She shook out the checkered cloth on the ground, opened a bottle of wine. Michael unwrapped the foil from a long loaf of bread. Claudina or Lester pulled out a Frisbee and moved off, under the power lines.

Even if the air was oppressively humid, with mists all over the sumac, Marimba could roll on her side and fall asleep.

Inside the house, Marimba's dog, Delaney, on waking up, yawned and shut his jaws, and ground his teeth, too.

He was an old dog—his mother a beagle, his father a terrier sort of mutt, and consequently Delaney could howl and Delaney could yap. He was as domesticated an animal as was Marimba, though neither of them knew how that happened, or quite what that meant for the future of the species.

Delaney never learned how to play dead, or how to beg, for which Marimba was grateful. He was bland in the presence of humans, steady-paced on walks, unabashedly curious about the ground and the life it harbored. He ate dirt, experimentally. He was a wary dog, not easily revolted. But easily pleased—too easily pleased, one might say: a chunk of hard-boiled egg could do it.

Delaney and Marimba had enough in common to regard each other, when they happened to regard each other, as two of a kind.

Before Marimba made an appointment to see anyone, she had already concluded: the problem is this—the human eyeball. The optical illusions of the mind. The illusion, for instance, which becomes the idea that one given moment follows another, discrete, self-contained—gold coins out of the mouth, filling a sack—giving time a shape. Here it is. The illusion that time is a human matter, and moves with us. Straight ahead. The illusion that we must proceed. And build. And keep an account. As if both the short and the long haul were ours, and ours, and not a careening, a warping, a folding over. Not the crush of the jaw. Not an exploding and a collapsing. As if the Alps were there, and there tomorrow, reservations available, and not, even now, sand for another flatbed sea.

Marimba's house, surrounded in the back by vacant fields, also faced a vacant field. Down the road, she could see the roofs of two trailers, and farther on, a red barn. Looking the other way, when leaves were off the trees and the scrub along the road had keeled over, she could see a corner of the house where Claudina and Lester lived.

Lester had dentures. Claudina had her own very good teeth, although when she laughed, her mouth opened wide and displayed a range of silver-alloy fillings, none of which she ever ground apart. Her motto, and explanation, was: ignorance is bliss. She could laugh about it. She could laugh at the evening news.

She could laugh at the men who hauled heavy equipment onto the field opposite Marimba's house, when the owner, nobody knew who, leased out mineral rights to a gravel company, in one of those exchanges of paperwork, dreamy as dream, that envisioned dollar bills in gravel in glacial dumps—those hills over there.

An earthmover—a mechanized steel jaw driven by one man—moved onto the field, and in several hours chewed out the side of the hill and built another. After that, a gravel-loader positioned itself against the opened hill and gutted it, with the enormous pummeling and crushing sounds of cartoon dreams.

When Claudina came to watch from Marimba's porch, she brought a half-gallon Ball jar of gin and tonic, a bowl of lime slices.

Since the business had turned into a show, Michael carried out dining room chairs. Marimba sat on the porch flooring and leaned into Michael, his legs like the arms of an easy chair on either side of her. She tried to lounge. She held his ankles in her hands. She listened to Claudina, who told the story of Lester's dentures.

But Marimba got through the hours mainly by viewing a sequence, fast motion, behind her eyes—a trick of the trick of the mind: she saw the steel tread and teeth of the earthmover stalled, ground into the ground; then taken over, a rapid decline, by rust, encrustations of lichen, encroachments, erosions, burials through various weathers, until the ground closed over completely; and Marimba was under there, too, and could see it. The weight of the earth and heat pressed the earthmover into the earth-as-it-moved. Buckled, melted, re-formed, re-moved as rock—it was and then it wasn't. Human things, all things after all, were down there, locked to the earth as it moved.

"Don't grind your teeth," Claudina was saying. "There's machinery now to do it."

And Marimba could see it was hard, emotionless work, annihilating what was.

An appointment with a hypnotherapist was set for Thursday. Late Wednesday afternoon, Michael and Marimba lay in bed. When Michael kissed her, his tongue traveled slowly along her teeth. Then his own front teeth, shapely ones, to her mind, settled on her lip, and she could feel the slight, exact space between them.

Across the road, the gravel-mining machinery roared in full gear. Michael talked loud.

"So, aren't you happy here?" he asked. He was naked, tan to his waist.

Marimba frowned. "This is fine!" She aimed her voice out the window. "It's that out there!"

"Well, something's bothering you."

"The world. That out there."

"But grinding your own teeth! Jesus. What's that do for the world? You hurt yourself. Feel that. Flat teeth." He leaned over, such a sweet person, and rubbed his finger between the bite of her teeth. He let himself down, the length of his weight resting easy, the way he could rest when he wanted to, very comfortable there on top of her.

His ear was close to her mouth, and she could whisper. "How about this? What if I tell the guy, 'This is a political problem. It's not personal.' How about that? It's true. I'll tell him a bad habit can be political."

The machinery outside geared up, working another hill. And, pretty generously, Marimba thought, she aimed her voice away from Michael's ear and shouted into the thicknesses of his hair. " 'You give me a decent world,' I'll tell him, 'I'll stop gnashing my teeth.' He'll take notes. He'll take notes, won't he? Mineral rights, gravel rights, dash, dash. Says noise of machinery, dash, dash, noise of attack! Rape! Defilement. Money extorted from the ground!"

"Good God," Michael said. "Shut the window."

She wore her white slacks instead of jeans, and sat with her legs slightly apart, at ease, as the man had suggested. Still, she was aware of a kink developing in one thigh.

The man lit a pipe. With her eyes shut, she could hear his breath in the stem of the pipe, and then the aroma of the tobacco moved in two channels of air she could picture clearly, around her head.

She thought it odd, thoughtless, really, that he'd smoke a pipe in a closed room, with a woman hypnotized in front of him.

Marimba made a note in her head to mention this point, when she opened her eyes. If he'd never thought of this behavior as a problem, what else hadn't he thought of?

Behind her closed eyes, Marimba watched. Kept track. She let her body sit like a well-placed shell, right there, in the chair opposite the man with the pipe.

When she'd first sat down, he'd asked her what she believed, specifically, to be the cause of her stress.

Specifically? She'd given him a list of things she'd noticed, driving to his office: the farm on Packard subdivided; the white stretch limo that passed her; two kids hounding a boy on a bike; all the headlines of all the papers; the design of his office building, a box of boxes; the geometric use of shrubbery, and so on.

He said, "Well, I see."

He said, "Find a spot to look at in the carpet, and just look. Just listen to me and look at the carpet."

Marimba had never thought very much of carpeting, in fact believed it to be another instance of a peculiarly human cover-up of the natural world, but she kept her mouth shut about that, and found a spot in the carpet, as instructed. She pretended the spot on the carpet was a chunk of dirt on the ground. And she stared at it for as long as he said.

. . .

Marimba explained to her mother at dinner, "He sucked his pipe. All the time my eyes were shut, he sucked his pipe!"

"Lots of men suck their pipes," her mother said.

"Well, it wasn't smart," Marimba insisted. "It's a very ignorant thing, in a hypnotherapist."

"He told her to give the world the finger," Michael said. "If you see an obscene gesture here, you'll see a posthypnotic suggestion at work. She's to do that instead of grinding her teeth."

"At night," Marimba said. "The suggestion is: display hostility rather than self-inflict it. Screw the world, he says. He says, You don't know how many men go around, surreptitiously giving their bosses the finger. He says it works. Releases the anger. Does no harm. He says this to me, Mother, while my eyes are shut, and he sits there sucking his pipe!"

"Oh, my darling," her mother said.

"I made notes," Marimba said, "for when I opened my eyes. I'd ask if he'd ever given thought to obscene gestures for women. Specifically for women. Could he see that women, physiologically, do not screw the world? I said, Give me an obscene gesture for women, and sure, I'd use it."

"Oh, baby doll," her mother said. "He's only been to school. You didn't expect miracles, did you? That's such a small world, all that. He probably lives in Ann Arbor. He probably went to school there. Lord," she said, "do you think it'll take?"

"I'll watch her at night," Michael said. "Keep clear of her arm."

"Hey, honey, I've got one!" Marimba's mother said. She stood up from the kitchen table. She held one hand in the air, a flourish, for effect, and made a fist. She pulled the thumb inside the fist, and brought the fist down.

"There! An obscene gesture for women," she said. "What do

you think, honey? Yank! Hey, the Yankee! You grab him, you got him. He's in your hand. A good fist! A powerful fist. What do you think?"

"It's not obscene," Marimba said.

"Well, all the better. Of course it's obscene! You just say so. Direct. Sexual. A woman's angle. Not abusive, not an attack, so that's even better. Michael, what do you think?"

"Good God. Don't ask me. It looks rough to me."

"That's good, then. It's a rough world," Marimba's mother said. "But Man-o-day, what a beauty." She yanked her fist down through the air again.

When Marimba ground out another filling, she told her dentist she wanted a hypnotherapist who knew about teeth. About the jaw. "That's all," she said. "I don't want to talk about anything else."

He referred her to a retired dentist who hypnotized as a hobby—a feeble man who wore a white dentist's coat.

They were in a dentist's office, the same as if she'd gone for a cavity. Marimba sat in the patient's chair, and the man tipped the chair back slightly. "Now," he said, "look at the ceiling."

It was a cheap tile ceiling, with shiny flecks scattered through the soundproofing material, silver and white. "Pick a spot," he said, "like a star." He turned his back. "Any spot."

Marimba stared at one fleck until her eyes watered, and the dentist said, "Now shut your eyes."

She knew the routine. She shut her eyes.

The dentist moved around the office, opening drawers, clinking metal objects against countertops, maybe cleaning up, Marimba thought, but why? She liked him, though, for walking around, and not sucking a pipe.

He said, "Now set your arm on the arm of the chair, wrist up. Like that. Now open your hand. Flex the fingers. Open your lips, too," he said. "Breathe easy. Let your palm breathe. Let the air go by your lips. It's very simple," he said.

"It's like saying hello when you want to say hello, don't you see?" he said. "There's an empty universe out there. You breathe into it. Say hello. That's about all you can do, sleeping. The rest of the time it is up to you, of course."

He shuffled some papers. "I'm leaving the office for five minutes," he said. "When I come back, your eyes will be open and you will feel fine."

The door shut. There was air-conditioning in the room, a hum of that machinery, and something else, maybe a clock. Marimba flexed the fingers of her right hand. Her jaw went slack. Air moved through her lips. She could hear it. The air of the universe, all right. There it was. The universe wasn't empty, she knew that. The air of the earth was not pure. But there it was.

"You can open your eyes now," the dentist said. His voice came from the hallway.

Marimba opened her eyes. "That wasn't five minutes," she said. "I was waiting five minutes to open my eyes."

The night of July the Fourth, not long after plum-size fireworks had disappeared from the horizon, Delaney the dog breathed a few times more loudly than usual, and died. Marimba and Michael listened to his chest, off and on, until they were both convinced there was nothing more there, and no chance.

They wrapped him in burlap and buried him under a tree.

The next morning—it was no surprise, really, that kind of

thing happens—something had got at Delaney's grave. The sod was kicked up, into a heap, and the burlap was ripped, pulled halfway out of the ground.

They dug a deeper hole, reburied Delaney; they stretched a section of chicken wire over the dirt as a barrier, set sod down again, and watered everything with a hose.

That time, he stayed put.

Through the summer, Marimba slept very well. The post-hypnotic flex system seemed to work, although Marimba didn't completely trust it. She kept a plastic mouthguard on hand, as a backup.

In the middle of the night, if Michael touched her on the arm, or on her thigh—well, if he touched her at all—she spat out the guard, and turned over to him. She kissed the mole on his chest first, and then she kissed his mouth. After that, even if the machines across the road were going at it, overtime, with floodlights on, one or the other of them managed to say, since they both liked to hear the words in the dark, "Listen. There's an empty universe out there."

Marimba could feel the words take shape in her mouth. She could hear them exit between her teeth.

ANTON'S
ALBUM

1   All right. In the grape arbor, and in the shadows, you can see me. He put me in there, just to look out. This is September, and he had forgot to prune in the spring. Look at the tangle.

2   The embassy, the rear door; and those are two bluebirds, one caught in flight, landing on the gravel the way they often do, tilting their wings and flashing that bluey blue. He's caught the corner of Geoffrey's car, accidentally, the gray blur over there.

3   That's not me, not on your life. That's Angelique. When he called the embassy and ordered up an angel, she's the one who showed.

4   Me again; I think this was the birthday dinner for Geoffrey. Anton called this shot Consideration. He asked me to bring
in the butter dish, and I only said, just like he would, "Give
me a chance to consider."

My hair was longer then, what a shame.

5   When Geoffrey moved out, Anton blamed the neighborhood. People with money were buying the houses, and there
were two seasons: sandblasting season and winter. Anton hated
it. "Literacy does this to a neighborhood," he said. "The bums
move out."

He took a picture when the couple across the street came
outside in coveralls to paint their wrought-iron fence.

6   These two, I'm not sure I can remember their names.
Anton ignored introductions; he had the idea that people would
make themselves known. These two stopped in about once a
year and brought tins of smoked salmon; and Anton took a day
off and we got some Bibb lettuce and cheese from Gaccione,
two blocks down. Gaccione'd say, "Tony, baby. Tony, you
deserve the best!" Always the same lip-smacking.

After a while, the wine bottles arranged themselves on the
table like bowling pins. These two guys, one was called Bob
White, I believe that was it, a bird's name, told long stories
involving motor troubles, leaking boats on the Yukon River,
and Anton would sit there tearing a lettuce leaf down the middle
and shaking his head side to side, "Oh, no, don't tell me."

I like the way they stood here, though, one behind the other, the same shoulders, like a two-headed man.

7   It's hard to believe, but this is Anton's mother. She came by train before Christmas that year, and when I kissed her cheek, she said, "I take it this is the child." From then on, she was like anybody else.

When I did her hair, Ice White, Anton took a picture, and she touched one hand behind her head and tipped up her chin, like a star.

8   Another picture of Anton's mother and me. Anton never made excuses—he wasn't a photographer. If somebody turned and the face washed out, that suited him. He said what he wanted was evidence.

"You two were here," he said about this one. "Here's the evidence."

9   Angelique again, in her blue dress, all the sequins. I'll tell you what I know about her. Her mother was Serbo-Croatian, and her father a Marriott-Hilton. She told this story as a way of accounting for how easily she could "dance in rooms—or not!" Then she howled, with her very smart laugh.

Anton was taken, I won't say smitten. He was taken. We had special foods, artichokes, fresh shrimp, red lettuce, asparagus with lemon grass and butter. Geoffrey did his work in the living room, reports on his lap, some secret, some not, he was just there, comfortable, out of the way, while Angelique put on music. I didn't mind. Why should I? I learned how to lounge, how to sprawl on a chair with upholstered arms, how to listen to anything, you name it.

Anton said, "What a sad life," talking about her; but he never would say it about himself.

10 And Geoffrey, in the arboretum. He came along as a favor, although he claimed no admiration for trees and no liking for gravel paths, which suggested corduroy to him, a texture he found unnatural. I gave him a walking stick—it was sassafras, and I peeled the bark off—and he sank his teeth into that, as I suggested, for a taste, before walking through the beech wood. By the time Anton took this picture, Geoffrey admitted there might be a pleasure or two, somewhere in the wild; and so he waved the walking stick, and he smiled. That's how simple he was.

11 True Value Hardware, that's right. This was my birthday, and my present was, I could take a picture anywhere I chose. Anton said, "Anywhere. You choose."

I said, "The place on the calendar."

And, very quick, Anton said, "And I say which calendar!"

If I had said one word—Crete, Lapland, anywhere—I'd have been there, to this day. It could have happened. Anton was not much for premeditation. His idea was, you could only think something through after the fact.

Since it was his present to me, I accepted. I'd forgot we had more than one calendar.

After the cake, instead of boarding a plane and flying to the Arctic Circle to take a picture, or flying to England, we took

Geoffrey's gray Olds over to Nebraska Avenue. The boxwood at the entrance to the store is sliced off the edge, just like the calendar picture, and the sun on the glass doors is about as bright.

12   I suppose this is Anton's favorite photo of the embassy, an incomprehensible picture, the heads of everybody lost off the top. But Anton said it was all right, he liked the colors. At the swimming party, the men posed in the pool, and here they are, the big shots, naked chest after chest after chest. They're columns of pink, peach pink, and the water is plain blue.

13   Geoffrey sent a picture of his room in Paris, the rue Victor-Cousin.

"Rue," Anton said. "Ruin." He gave me the photograph to throw in the wastebasket.

It was a dark room, if I remember correctly, with the camera aimed out the window toward the rooftops across the street, with some of the windows over there shuttered and some open.

Anton decided to take this picture, out the front window of our place, with the frame of the window the frame of the picture, and the roof of the house across the street cutting a low triangle, green-shingled, and the white sky above it, all around, very bright, your large city sky, no color, probably ozone.

You can see, though, he never sent the picture to Geoffrey. He kept it here.

14   All right, look. Here he is. Nothing I can say will show you Anton better than this, enthroned, on the back porch in

the ratty gold chair. That's not his Amish hat, that's mine, to match my hair, and Geoffrey took this picture.

These are all out of order.

This was the summer, and we were celebrating Independence Day, waiting for the fireworks, doing nothing the way we did it best.

Anton set up the tripod, the timer, and tried to take a picture of the three of us, arranged, he said, so that nobody outshone anybody else, but it didn't work. After a couple of foul-ups, Anton picked my hat off my head and said to Geoffrey, "There's one shot left. Take me."

He sat back in the chair, the wide-brimmed hat on his head. In the shade, he grinned with his eyes, but you can see the uneven tips of his front teeth, which hardly anybody ever saw.

It's a good picture. That's how he looked that afternoon. This was a lucky shot, and I'm lucky to have it because usually Anton wasn't very good at looking good.

15   Here is the old woman who moved into Geoffrey's car in the alley for three nights. She didn't speak English. Anton finally gave up pointing at the door.

16   There aren't any other pictures, those last months. Anton stopped taking pictures. I was ready for it when he told me to leave, I should be on my own. I kissed his fingers.

I said, "What's far away?"

"Calcutta," he said. "Anchorage. How about a ticket to Anchorage?" His mouth stayed open.

"One way to Anchorage, that's fine."

"It's not a pretty place," he said.

I let my mouth sag, too, and didn't say anything. I just looked back at him until he said, the way I always say it, "All right."

At the airport, I asked if I could take a picture, and Anton rolled down the car window and looked out. He didn't look pretty, not that day. I took this picture, though, and I'm glad he let me take it. I took his album, too, out of the living room rubble.

I wouldn't take anything else. I owe him too much. His idea was, it was the same with humans as with God: after you saw the ruin, that's all there was. The rest didn't matter. The idea pleased him, when it didn't make him ugly. And it pleases me, too.

MARGUERITE
LANDMINE

Marguerite took her show on the road, a last tour, to end at the Capitol, where the senior senator from Rhode Island had arranged a performance for the combined houses. Outside Wheeling, Marguerite pulled off the highway and climbed into the back of the van, where she pulled her arrival costume from a plastic bag in the drawer numbered 1. She changed in the brief moment it took a tractor-trailer to approach the van, rush by with a dramatic waffling of winds, and reduce itself to a small square ahead, which continued reducing itself to the east. It's possible the driver never saw the van, with its sides and doors painted the legendary colors and shapes of Blue Ridge Mountain.

Over the years, Marguerite had found innovative ways to transport her props and equipment, even the most elaborate sets, in the small compartments of the van, which she painted and repainted in rented garages, city to city. In interviews, Marguerite acknowledged the van as an accomplice, nondescript, the one that effected the fabulous disappearances she'd managed all her life. She didn't acknowledge much else.

Rhode Island claimed Marguerite, because the state figured so fully in her performances; but the archives revealed no record of birth or residence there, and Marguerite preferred to ignore specifics. "I was spat from a pond's eye," she said. Or sometimes she said, "I was spat from my mother's eye."

And she looked it.

In her arrival costume, a dragonfly draping arrangement of fabrics and papers, whoever she was in herself was no longer a matter of interest. There was no discerning. She worked her own metamorphoses, not with the leisure of nature but with the jolt and high-voltage twist of machinery, a shock like the stamping of sheet metal into a car door, the electronic *ping* of soldering, microscopic—a mime of state-of-the-art technologies. Her paraphernalia folded and self-compacted, and opened up at a touch.

Marguerite called herself, in some states, Marguerite Origami, she had such skill, such constructive know-how. Engineers working to make it big in the pop-up-book business studied her sets; and it was with as much generosity as arrogance that in book towns Marguerite flung out some of her work into the crowd, the miniature pieces with smooth, curved edges and a fullness of body, the texture of skin, the folds and collapses of paper—and the engineers said it *was* paper—imperceptible.

But elsewhere, her posters announced: Marguerite Landmine; Marguerite Prefab; Marguerite Rhode Island.

Crossing the new and reconstituted Tuscarora Range, with its elaborate hangings and camouflages, with its wide-spanning palmlike pines developed for the East, Marguerite felt the pain in her legs that had recently signaled trouble. First came the hints, the alarms, of the pain, and then, up from the feet, an encroaching blankness, a loss of touch. She slowed the van and kicked each leg at the knee. The nutmeg, autumnal scent of her boots lifted through the wrappings of costume. The pain held off. She pressed the accelerator to the floor.

Housing developments, roof to roof, under the palm and finger pines, slurred by the window, and driveways blinked short spans of asphalt, broken lines on either side. The van streamed down the road, a bit of scenery on the loose. This was the way Marguerite advised her fans to travel, in the guise of landscape, since there was none; in the recollection of Rhode Island, the ancient place, whose name now had assumed such mystery.

Marguerite was speeding. Soon enough she heard the sirens of police in pursuit. She exercised her knees once more, and pressed the accelerator with renewed force. In the rearview mirror, however, she saw it was not the police, not a battery, but one motorcycle cop, and she adjusted the mirror for a better look. She eased her foot from the pedal.

What she thought she had seen, she easily verified: the cop wore no ballooning helmet, no gloves. He was not regulation. She watched his fingers comb and push at his hair, which was long enough to blow in strips across his face. His motorcycle veered with this gesture, and she saw, instantaneously, as if she had contrived it herself, the steel plates of the motorcycle snap into gold, a textured gold, like the straw of old hats, the straw still found in the last barns, in the deserts.

Marguerite pulled onto the shoulder. She watched in the mirror. "Little van, he's a beauty," she said. She could see the flesh on his wrists. She hummed to herself, "Oh, Rhode Island . . . dum de dum . . ."

He parked the motorcycle behind the van and loosened his orange police vest, straightened his shoulders. In the rearview mirror, Marguerite watched as he raised an arm and waved at her, like a boy, in that circle. She watched his hair blow around his face in the gusts from passing vehicles, and she noticed he touched the side of the van as he approached, as a person might touch, tentatively, a pond surface nowadays, to test if the pond was a water pond.

At her window, he said, "They told me you couldn't be stopped." He put his hands on the window ledge, all of his fingers inside the van, and Marguerite breathed on them.

"That's right, I can't," she said.

"You're still on your way, then," he said, and he extended one hand inside the van, toward her hand, the old-fashioned greeting.

Marguerite took his hand, and the fragrance of skin, so much more complicated than any perfuming, swept through the van, and she leaned back in the seat, to inhale. The boy, too, pulled back for a second, and then pressed his other hand over hers and breathed an open-mouth breath, like a sigh.

"You haven't lost your senses!" Marguerite said.

"No!" he said.

"Get in!" she said.

With the windows rolled up, the traffic outside withdrew, a muffled sound, distant, oceanic, with tidal approaches and declines. The boy took off the orange police vest, and they sat there, apart, touching each other's arms, the fine hair on the arms. With both hands, each pressed the skin along the curve of the other's jaw, and touched the ridged, tendoned sides of the neck, following the collarbone's slight angle until the skin warmed toward the center of the body, and the fingers of their hands met there, pendent, and Marguerite's arms and the boy's arms lay beside each other, between each other, like the lengths of bodies.

When Marguerite opened the boy's shirt, it shook in her hands and crumpled away into folds, like her own fabrications, designed not for wear but for dismantling. The boy pulled the thread on her shoulder which separated her costume into its patterned sections, and lightweight, the papers settled against the door, blown there by their breathing. Every breath, though easy and silent, brought with it the rustle of onionskin, feather, crepe paper, and foil.

"I knew your skin would be like this," he said, and he pressed his cheek against her belly. He took her hands and wound them around his back until the palms of her hands, on their own, felt their way along his spine and down the sides of his back, down his thighs.

They rolled themselves into the open space, the small room of the van.

"You are scenic!" Marguerite said. And she traced the veins in his arms the way she had traced on antique maps the rivers of Rhode Island.

When they kissed, the boy touched the slope of her breasts and the ledge of her knees.

He rubbed her legs, he wrapped them in his. They stretched out beside each other and worked themselves into and out of tangles. They languished; they kept pace. All afternoon, the noise of their bodies continued, primordial, with something of rock and something of water in it.

Outside, to the passing traffic, the van and the motorcycle, in their fantastic colorations, appeared, if they appeared at all, like a billboard, a painted picture of bygones—a straw bale in a field, and there, as backdrop, the shadow, the rise of Blue Ridge Mountain.

When they pulled apart, only their toes and their fingers touching, Marguerite said, "This time, I've made birds exactly like birds. And creatures. But—no!" She reached for her ankles, as the pain entered there, and then, with a sharper pain, drained away. Marguerite gripped her ankles, but they were not there, not to the touch.

The boy rubbed her feet and kissed them and rubbed them again.

He said, "Let me drive."

Marguerite, with a flick of her arms, drew on her costume, and the boy dressed, too.

She rested her feet in the boy's lap, and as he drove, he held them there, scuffed them, and worked to keep the legs warm.

"It's no better," she said.

At the Capitol, the boy backed the van up to the loading dock, and while Marguerite sat with her hands on her knees, her eyes shut, he greeted the representatives and carried cartons onto the stage.

When the houselights dimmed, the boy walked Marguerite onto the stage, his arms supporting her. She withdrew the hand-made birds from small cages and loosed them. Several senators stood up, to catch the prizes. And as the elaborate sets opened up, one after another, the house filled with the noise of paper and soaring.

For a time, the boy watched the show as if Marguerite were elsewhere, not in his arms.

Four-legged creatures advanced from the wings and fed on corn. Birds flew through a Rhode Island wilderness, into the cities, and out again, to the distant swamplands.

"I must kiss your neck," Marguerite said. "The terrain—the terrain," she whispered, "is so beautiful."

Then he felt the weight, no longer buoyant, of her body. He felt her arms fall. He tore the brittle papers away, to let her skin breathe and warm next to his. He pumped the air from his lungs in and out, like a bellows.

When the crowd's attention turned from the birds and the unfolding scenery to Marguerite at the side of the stage, she lay like a woman, sleeping with a lover.

The members of Congress remained silent a moment, attentive.

Then, of course, they applauded: Marguerite Origami had so perfectly made a man, and a contraption in her own shape, there in his arms.

THE EASTER
WE LIVED
IN DETROIT

The best day I remember was the Easter we lived in Detroit, locked in the apartment all day. The furniture, the rugs, began to breathe. Geraniums hummed. I thought, so this is a lively place. It's what happens when somebody's got a chance to think.

Early, about seven o'clock, I said to my husband, Loren, It's bright out, which was at first a complaint. But Loren can sleep with the sun in his eyes; he didn't wake. I believe it's more natural, though, with the eyes closed, to be in the dark, and that is why, very deliberately, when the sunlight compressed itself from a general glow to a four-cornered field next to the bed, I got up and pulled down the green shades in both rooms. The floorboards were cool or warm, depending on where I stepped, and checking around, I found a warmed-up spot near the living room window, where I stood for a while with my feet pressed flat, so the heat moved upwards through my ankles.

My feet are spongy and pale, the white kind of feet that sculptors put at the ends of women's legs. I know what luxury-living means, soaking them in the sun.

In the kitchen, I took a blue-painted hard-boiled egg from the refrigerator, poured some milk, and let my eyes travel the walls in the indoor light. It was a greenish, undersea light, very mild. I peeled the egg and sliced it with a steak knife onto a big plate, where the two halves slid together. They arranged themselves, it certainly seemed to me then, as downhearted, pitying eyes. I just whispered, Don't you worry. Not today.

The air was unusually pretty, iridescent. The watercolor light of the room washed into the milk and swirled some pastels. The white of the egg shone aquamarine. Through the plumbing, or through the floors, I heard the rush of water falling, and I washed the knife, to add to it, and even after I'd set the knife off to one side to dry, I let the water run, full force, from the faucet into the drain, for somebody's pleasure down below. Noises coming from far away, I decided then, the ones that have nothing to do with your own life, can be more important than anything anyone says in your own ear. It may be for that kind of reason, too, I turned on the radio, for the noise of the Easter broadcasts, a Sunday sound that seemed to come from a great distance and out of some other scenery. I've advised Loren, many Sundays, Listen, they're dreamy. You shouldn't mind it, I tell him. Let them pursue happiness, that's what I say about that. But he won't listen.

For Easter, 92 Rock was given over to a man with a damaged, smoker's voice who read haltingly, like a beginning reader, the story about the women at the tomb, where the rock had rolled away, making a space as wide as a door. I kept the sound low and listened off and on; and since I knew the story anyway, I could picture very clearly the roundness of the rock and the dark hole in the hill. It was desert there, with no trees, and the soil thin and shallow, with bedrock practically under your feet, so that caves were used as tombs. Or was it for criminals only that caves were tombs? I don't recall ever hearing the full explanation.

I sat in the kitchen eating the egg. With the radio on and the light in the rooms going green to gold, the morning just lulled—it held itself steady, unattached to things in the room, and I tell you I sat with my back against the back of the chair, content as a queen who, when the palace was ransacked, carried off her own throne and set it somewhere in the woods. She was worn out; she didn't have a thing; but there she was.

I chewed and swallowed and let the cells of my brain go to work. I thought, this is an opportunity. You can't think in bed. You can't think on the radio. But I sat still, and the less I moved, the more I noticed how, one after another, the thoughts lined up, linked themselves, and ran together like frames of a moving picture. I sat there and let it happen.

Of course, in the past, I had given thought to a number of things. I'd thought about Loren, who'd lost, or surrendered, the use of his hands. I'd thought about that, from all the angles. And with the *Free Press* delivered every day, I paid attention to events, foreign or domestic, violent or nonviolent, since it all counts in the end. And, lately, I'd also tried to decide how it happened that during the winter our daughter, Patty, had made me a grandmother at thirty-four—but that was a simple matter of arithmetic. And not so surprising, considering she'd run off from school the day before Thanksgiving vacation with the evangelical Mr. Stutz, the book burner with the megaphone, the one the *Free Press* called the Noisemaker. The paper said in one article that Patricia Dove, 224 N. Grand River, described this Mr. Stutz as "a person you trust through and through."

What is harder to understand, when you think about it, is the fact that I didn't know, as of Easter, if the grandchild was boy or girl—I'd never seen it, and never would see it, because Patty was keeping the child for God. *Harboring* was her word on the phone. I am harboring the child for God. I'd thought after that about harboring, about crimes perpetrated, one way and another.

All of this thinking led nowhere. It knotted up. My mind kept a list of concerns, a mix, like a canned-soup label with a long paragraph of ingredients, so that you wonder as you taste it if all those things are really necessary.

But the Easter we lived in Detroit, it was a clear, surging day from the start, with fair-weather clouds crossing the window square above the sink.

It was easy to look around. To the right of the living room door, on the metal radiator cover, was the spider plant; and to the left, on a shelf, was Patty's junior picture, in a cardboard frame—she had her father's straight brown hair, parted in the middle. From where I was, with a slow, continuous turning, I could take in the sofa, which was red plaid, a decent-looking thing, where Loren usually sat to watch TV, and on through the bedroom door I could see Loren's feet at the end of the bed, his toes pointing up, slightly outward. I could look at his feet. Separate objects in the rooms, even though I kept them separate and shadowed with thick lines like the crayon lines of a child's drawing, were nonetheless part of a train of thought. Even a small thing—a book, or a scrap of dust in the corner—took up a quantity of space, and the room seemed full of things to be seen and space to be seen between. When I looked at something, I saw it. I noticed on the wall space next to the front door the old photograph of my grandmother standing in a yard beside a little pine tree, holding me, her youngest grandchild, a baby over her shoulder. The frame was oval, gold metal. In the picture, my head was blurred, turned away, and smudged into the sky of the background. I decided: this is a picture of the pine tree, that's what. I was glad to know it. Count the years, you can figure the tree has grown into something huge, very dark, in somebody's backyard. It is probably so dark, day or night, it looks like empty space.

I decided if I saw Patty again, I'd give her the picture.

On the radio, the man's voice stumbled, mispronouncing *sepulchre*—you'd have thought it was a brand-new story for him. He coughed, trying to cover up, and went on.

Years ago, when Patty was a child small enough to hold on one arm, I remember holding her on Christmas morning and telling her it was the day Jesus was born, and she said, very sweet and mournful in my ear, yes, she'd heard about him, she'd heard they put him in a tube. A *tube*! Well, you can understand that when she was swept up last fall with the Noise-maker, I thought I'd lighten things up and remind her of her first Christian knowledge.

But she couldn't laugh. She said, Mother, shame.

What's shame? I said. I tell you a funny joke, I said.

But Patty's a serious girl; she always was.

A choir sang. I stretched my legs and shoulders, crackling vertebrae in my back, and I remembered I hadn't got the paper yet from the hall. With the midmorning noises from outside—cars braking for the light and gunning off, a whistling kettle across the alley—I could move around easily without waking Loren. I unlocked the front door, picked up the paper, and locked the door again. Even while it was folded, I could see the paper had a very predictable three-color picture on the front page, of a mountainside near Jerusalem, where a touring dramatic club had staged an Easter pageant. Except for a winged angel who sat at one side, the scene came close to the one of the tomb I had pictured myself.

After the headlines, I slid myself back into bed, where the sheets on my side had cooled, and I pushed against Loren, curling myself to his back like a shadow, which he had occasion to notice, and he said, Here, Mummy, here you go. He rolled over to me with what I would call real intent. I don't deny that I had been thinking, too, a kind of a thought: dear God, a double bed and two bodies in it—Easter—and no place to go.

Loren was forty-two. He claimed his hands were dead hands, although they were very beautiful, and patterned with veins and with crisscrossed lines in the shape of stars on his knuckles. Sometimes he let his hands hang from his wrists as if they'd been chopped off and reattached with a hidden stitching. Every day he would set the hands flat on the tabletop and look at them. With a snap of his elbows, he'd flip the hands over and examine the palms. They looked fine to me. But he'd study them as if anytime he expected them to move against his will. I think he'd prepared himself to recalculate, at the moment that happened, everything he knew. He didn't use the word *miracle*, but I think he believed one had already hit him, and that possibly it would happen again and undo itself.

If he'd been another person, instead of himself—Loren, a welder—Loren, Patty's father—he might have been able to figure out what was what. But being the man he was, he veered. He wasn't a bitter man, but he couldn't put two and two together. He learned to stare. When he saw something going on, when he saw Patty pack up the red suitcase and leave, for example, he stood in the doorway and flicked his head as if he were snapping his welder's helmet in place, and having trouble with it. But he didn't blink; and he didn't say anything more than good-bye.

By Easter, I'd allowed myself to admit that I lived with a vacated Loren, a shadowy man who'd discovered silence and who made love much more carefully now.

Loren liked to read the paper, and he read every column, including the ones in the business section. After I gave him breakfast, he sat with the paper in his lap, the back pages propped against the table. While he read and while the radio man talked on, I washed dishes. From the kitchen, I didn't mind watching him. The past can cut itself off very smoothly. It's possible that Loren's life from birth had been surrounded with a silence nobody noticed, and I certainly never noticed, until he stopped working. But then the quiet accumulated; it polished him, waxy and definite. That Easter morning, at a distance of twenty feet, I could see the capsules, like layers of color, around him. I took some time, looking at him. I watched him the way you watch, unpitying, an insect going its own way in the alley, working its legs over chucks of gravel. You feel lucky just to see it.

"It's the Noisemaker," Loren said. "Here's where she is." He nodded and pointed with his forehead to an article in the paper.

I read over his shoulder. It was a brief note: Richard Stutz, 28, arraigned for trespassing, breaking and entering, and malicious destruction of property, after an incident at the Allegan High School. Rock-and-roll records, brand-name articles of clothing, books—some of them stolen out of the library—had been heaped on a bonfire in the schoolyard. Apparently Mr. Stutz had broken a window in the library, climbed in, and

thrown out selected titles. The article didn't mention his megaphone, but I knew it was there, calling from inside the building,
describing each step, naming each book as he pulled it off the
shelf. There was no mention of Patty; I didn't expect any. She'd
have been somewhere out of sight. And nothing about the
Noisemaker's baby.

"She's in Allegan," Loren said.

"I'll look it up."

On the Rand McNally map, Allegan was marked in the
western fruit-growing area, a greenish strip with gray hatching.
The whole section was stamped with small, rounded trees, the
symbol for orchards and vineyards.

"Drop her a line," Loren said. "Maybe in care of the court-
house?" He pushed at the paper and flipped the page.

The letter was simple to write. I wasn't very hopeful about
it, one sheet of paper, but I knew it wouldn't hurt.

In the living room, bright streaks from the sun came in around
the shades, and I snapped them up and let the daylight in, a
liquidy milk sort of light that flowed across the room, straight
for the table. But it was cool, and I moved the typewriter from
the sewing table into the lighted space opposite Loren. Without
planning ahead what to say, I started in, typing at my top speed,
which is above average, and which Loren sometimes smiles at,
as if the tapping noise and the running of fingers from key to
key means something special to him.

I can tell you exactly what I wrote, because I have the letter
here. It came back after a month. Someone had opened it up
and taped it shut, I don't know who.

I told Patty it was Easter and did she remember that. I told
her just because she was in the orchards and not in a desert

region not to feel left out of it all, that I didn't. Loren, at this point, said to say hello, and I typed in: Patty, your father says hello.

When I saw those words, I knew that Patty, because of the Noisemaker, would think about God the Father, that's how she thinks, and that is why I went on with this talk about her father. I told her, Your father is right here, across the table from me. You know who I'm talking about. You know who your father is, I told her. And I know who your baby's father is, Richard Stutz. Think about this, Patty. I am your mother, and you are your baby's mother. My guess is, I told her, the baby is a boy. I asked her point-blank. I am your mother, and I ask you, Patricia, would you harbor a girl for God? Oh, no, I told her. You were *my* little girl, I told her, and I harbored you for *nobody*. Look at yourself. You're grown up. I told her to sit down in the sunlight somewhere to read the letter and remember, as she well knew, that she was a daughter of mine and of her father, that's whose. God doesn't want your baby any more than God wanted you. I tried to say it plain. I told her I didn't know where she was but I thought she should walk the baby boy on the beach and tell it who its father and mother were, and who its grandmother and grandfather were. Tell him his grandmother has new white-capped teeth, better than anything you'd believe, and that his grandfather says hello from Detroit. Sit in the sand all afternoon, I told her, and think. I told her, do you really believe God has the chance to think the way we do? None of this will surprise you, I said. We are thinking of you. Your father, who is no better, is also no worse, and he says, fare thee well—which he did say. I said, Be well, my dearest one. With love, your mother.

. . .

Loren and I finished reading the paper. At noon, he took a nap, which went on all afternoon. I opened the living room window and sat on the sill, listening to the radio. The window had no screen; I could open it wide and sit there, watching the space over the roofs, where the light held on. It was a pale light that slowed people down and hushed them up. Kids on bicycles riding no-hands swerved smoothly and turned up the alley as if their bikes were on automatic. Nobody shouted to anybody.

For supper, I cooked a steak, and we watched the news on TV. A reporter outside a crumbled building in Jerusalem said that no incidents of violence disrupted the Christian holiday.

"No violence here, either," I said to Loren.

He shook his head.

After the news, I turned on the radio again and we had our ice cream. Loren went to the window. On the radio a preacher was saying, it fills us with amazement, *amazement*, he said, that Jesus rose up from the arms of death. He was dead, he was in the tomb, but he rose up.

Loren sat down on the sill with his arms in his lap and watched the street. Listen, Mummy, he said. Turn off the radio. Look.

I turned it off and walked over beside him. There were sirens. A haze wound itself over the city, gauzy and pinkish orange.

Loren leaned back against the window frame and I sat opposite. I told him I'd had a whole day to study what was on my mind, and see, I came on through it. I told him it didn't surprise me that a person who knew what God knew, given the time to think, would throw over the idea of staying dead, and come back, and keep on going.

Loren said, Hold my hand. I took his hand and I held it up to my mouth. All of his fingers pointed to the ground. The skin on his arm was soft, untanned, with fine brown hair, and I drew my tongue across the hairs.

The sirens moved in and then came blue flashing lights, headed downtown. Patty's letter lay somewhere behind me, in the middle of the table, sealed and stamped. Loren and I sat on the windowsill while the dark took over the living room and took over the ground outside, too. The dark, which is like a shelter around each person, is a lovely thing to see, once you see it.

THE SKY
IS STILL
OVERHEAD

When that particular sky—and I'll get to it—splayed itself over the car, and out from there to the horizon, low on all sides, that was when Sylvia took off her dark glasses, looked around, and rolled down the window for some air.

She said, I haven't changed my mind, Mr. Watson. Nothing has changed.

She stuck to all the formalities. But she listened. She was willing to take the time for a business discussion.

If I worried about her, it was because of her eyes, and not the eyes themselves but the blue or purple-blue under her eyes, a natural enough color, that's true—the color of low-pressure skies, March skies—but too much a painted effect, even though it wasn't painted, on the skin. She looked made-up.

When she sat still, and leaned back, she looked like a woman posed for a portrait, for Max Beckmann, and already painted there on canvas.

She looked like a woman capable of harm.

If this were Beirut or Bologna, a man with money would not talk to this woman.

She would have a weapon. She would have nothing but bitterness in her voice, and she wouldn't disguise it.

But this is a different world. And the sky I am talking about is a U.S.A. sky. It could have come with a label.

Sylvia said, The air smells like mud.

Water, I said.

The lake was there, down the hill. But she was right: the air that came in the car window, the air that blew down from the sky, carried a marly smell, as if other lakes, overhead, swamp lakes, floated up there out of sight and contributed to the direction, the composition of wind. The wind held the clouds up, or dropped from them, and leveled along the ground until the pattern, west to east, kicked up a flow of air that filled whatever room there was between clouds and ground.

The clouds—these particular clouds—were flat-bottomed puffs, scuffed up at the edges, and ranged in tight rows, a couple of brush strokes each: gray going to blue on the underside, gray going to white toward the tops.

Outside every window of the car, the same scene. Very painterly. Almost too pretty.

Wind blew against the metal of the car and funneled itself in through Sylvia's open window.

She said, When you talk about money, how much are you talking about?

I gave her the round figures. A fair price.

And if I don't sell?

I told her, fine. The lots were zoned. She'd be surrounded anyway, it didn't matter to me.

Then she said she could always set fire to her house goddamn-it, that it didn't matter to her.

That's one way to do business.

I told her that.

The car door whistled, and Sylvia opened the door, slammed it shut, to fix it. But the thing whistled again.

Then she got out and walked off a bit. She sat on a rock at the edge of the parking space. The wind blew her hair forward over each ear. A part in her hair opened up, wind-combed, almost white, straight up the back of her head.

The Midwest is a godforsaken place, I'm happy to say it. There's plenty of room to expand. Business looks like it might actually turn around. What I should do is build, just build. It's the buying and selling that gets to me. These poor souls with muck in their hearts. Brick houses worth shit. She'd have a hard time burning that down.

But then, this is not a violent country. Sylvia isn't stupid. I'd say, in fact, she enjoyed the weather. As much as I did. The particulars of the sky. She noticed it all.

There is so much prettiness in the world, even when days are rough, you can see it.

Sometimes I surprise people with that word: prettiness. I use it. It's a word I am known to use, even in this business. An antique word, but what the hell. I wouldn't say beautiful. I don't think I've ever said something is beautiful.

Sylvia sat on the rock in the wind and said nothing.

The edge of the rock had been hammered off—it was clean-grained and blue inside. I split a rock like that with a sledge when I was a kid. It was a shock, to see so much color. I see it all the time: the world is a colorful place, not worn out, not all of it made out of dirt and the color of dirt. Rocks on the surface of any field jut up pale, and they rest there—that's how it looks—in their preparation to crumble to dirt—dirt-brown, dirt-red.

But you split a rock and it's blue, bluer than this one, blue among shards like mirrors. Or pink. Or green. Or anything. Mirrors and blue stone. You never know.

Sylvia eventually got the picture. She was sour, but who wouldn't be.

She said, The sun will fry the planet up, I am counting on that. Which is why, she added next, it is possible to be kind.

That's not, I told her, the only possibility.

Oh, she said. I could pick up a rock and crack your head, is that a possibility?

She picked up a rock. And of course that's how quick a man can straighten his back. I grabbed some air in both hands, that's how it felt. I thought, The sky is still overhead. The rock is blue, inside.

But under that particular rock, there they were, very neatly folded—two green dollar bills.

Sylvia saw them, too, first thing. She set the rock aside. She picked up the money. Next to the bills lay some coins, pressed in the dirt. She counted them out.

These must be yours, she said.

Some kid's buried treasure, I told her. I kicked at the rock. I looked out over the lake. A slab of ice floated just about in the middle, marbled, shining with cloud shapes.

Well, give it some thought, I said. You could afford, I told her, a place on the water.

She walked toward me. Her arm came up. On her little finger she had a whitish ring, a bone ring. Or ivory.

Here, Sylvia said. It's yours.

She handed the money over. Two dollars and sixty-five cents.

What the hell, I took it.

NEWS

Smiley walked down the road and into Rochelle's kitchen for the first time in six years, a return visit Smiley called it, and there she was, in white shorts, sitting on a stool at the freestanding counter Rochelle called an island.

"You picked a day," Rochelle said. She stood with a knife in her hand. She looked around. No point in cleaning up. No point in trying. On the island and on the counters lay fifteen plucked chickens, half with the feet on, half without; a few gutted, most not. And everywhere else, chicken parts: a pan of livers and hearts on the island. Yellow stalks of feet piled on a brown paper bag. And in the sink, a large bowl of loopy intestines, crops, an esophagus like a white plastic tube.

"There's five more to go," Rochelle said. "That's it."

"I don't mind," Smiley said. "There's been plenty of chicken death in my family, as you know. Soup is the ticket. We're fifth-generation Campbells. Me and the kids could be rich, you know. We're in line to inherit, if we outlive the right people." Smiley twisted her bare legs around the legs of the stool and made herself comfortable.

"If you squint," Rochelle said, pointing toward the sink, "there's beauty there. The colors."

Smiley didn't squint.

"On the other hand," Rochelle went on, "it's devastation. It's the mire."

In the air of the kitchen, she knew it, in the cloth of her shirt, hung the surgical smell of singed feathers, the open-body smell of carcasses.

"Honey, you have a thread of something, there in your hair," Smiley said.

Rochelle combed at her curls with her fingers. "God only knows," she said. She threw something into the sink.

At the back door, Joe gave two kicks, and when Rochelle opened the door for him, he bowed and held out five more chickens, upside down, three in one hand, two in the other. "Where do you want these?"

With his elbow, he shoved a kettle to one side of the island and stacked the chickens in the open space. He washed his hands in a corner of the sink.

"Well, it's about time!" he said to Smiley. "I don't believe it." He took her hand and kissed her cheek. "How are you? It's luck you stopped by, I tell you. How are you?"

"Unlucky. Why else would I stop in? I come in misery, I'm ready to belt my kids, and I walk in here and Rochelle has her hands bloodied and I think, what has happened to poor Joey?"

"Not to worry," he said. "Joey is intact. Rochelle gives the slaughter order, and slaughter it is. No mercy."

"They look nice," Smiley said. "You'll have plenty of meat."

"We didn't kill them for meat," Rochelle said. "We killed them to get rid of them. These are murdered chickens. We'll eat them, but they are murdered chickens."

"Murder?" Smiley said. "You murdered chickens?"

"Rochelle, for God's sake. Have a beer," Joe said. "You want a beer, Smiley?"

"I can't drink a beer in here," Rochelle said. But she put down the knife and washed her hands, too.

"So come outside," Joe said. "Take a break."

"It's worse out there."

"We will do *this*," Smiley said. She took the three beers Joe handed out from the refrigerator. "We will go onto the front steps, where we can watch the road and see no blood and think no blood and we will all be fine." She pushed against the screen door with her shoulder and held the door open. "Let the flies *in*, and we will go out."

It was July, a cloudless late afternoon with no wind. They sat on the top step of the porch. Joe leaned his back against the doorjamb, shook some dark feathers off his T-shirt, and pulled Rochelle by the hand until she sat down beside him. Smiley sat with her legs crossed. She did a few waist bends, side to side. Her hair was short, bleached very blond, and when she leaned over, yellow hair fell across her face in a fringe.

"Did you hear the news?" she said. "They got a woman nominated?"

"Absolutely," Rochelle said.

"And *that*," Joe said, "I tell you, accounts for the end of these chickens."

"Not completely," Rochelle said.

"Completely," he said. "When did you say you had enough?"

"Yesterday."

"And when did you hear the news?"

"Yesterday."

"I'm not kidding," Joe said. "It touched us very close."

Rochelle watched a bee, upside down in a red petunia.

"You think that's why I nearly clobbered my kids?" Smiley stood up and did a few knee bends. She touched her toes.

"You got problems with your kids?" Joe asked.

"Randolph. He's sixteen, this month, and he says he has to see Wyoming, and to see Wyoming he has to take the Chevette."

"Let him go," Joe said. "He's a good kid."

"I told him, I know exactly what you're after—more dope and less oxygen, and he says to me, lady, you are crazy. He says, I don't do dope! Well, I said, I certainly don't know, but I know this, if I were *you*, if I were a boy your age, it would certainly be at the top of *my* list. So he says, all I want to know is, can I have the Chevette?"

"He's a good kid," Joe said. "You're too rough on him."

"Joe's vocation," Rochelle said, "is solving household problems."

"Well, we got twenty dead chickens," Joe said. "We solved one here."

When they heard the news on the TV, Rochelle clapped her hands over her head. "For a couple of days," she said, "that woman will not have one problem."

"And I suppose you have problems," Joe said. He stuffed a pillow behind his head and sat up a little in the bed.

"No, not really."

"Well, I *like* a woman with problems," he said. "There's something to do there, and I'm good at problem solving."

"The problems that you can solve aren't problems," Rochelle said. "The problems that I've *got* aren't problems."

"And what does that mean? If there's a solution, there's been a problem."

"What I mean is, the problems that you can solve don't count. They don't matter." Rochelle got out of bed. "Do you want some toast or something?"

"Sure. Toast is good. It'll solve the problem of my hunger."

"A problem that doesn't count," Rochelle said. She turned off the TV. "You know what I'm talking about. Problems. The ones that have no solutions."

"There's no such thing."

"Mayhem," Rochelle said. "Horror, madness, you name it." They went downstairs.

"Those are facts," Joe said, behind her. "They happen."

"And is love a fact or a problem? I ask you, matter-of-fact," Rochelle said.

"Cut it out, Rochelle." He put two slices of bread in the toaster. "It's sure as hell not mayhem." And he smiled and let Rochelle take account of his eyes smiling, too—he meant what he said.

"Well, what are some problems you solve?"

"Name a problem you've got," he said.

"One that you can solve, you mean."

"I don't know. Just name one."

"We don't count money as a problem. That doesn't count," she said.

"All right. Forget money. Name me one problem."

"The chickens. What about them?"

"Good. There. There's a problem," Joe said. "All right now. What's the solution?"

"That's your problem."

"All right. The chickens are vicious. They peck each other. That's normal. They've done some damage."

"They *assault* each other," Rochelle said. "One's dead. They've pulled out half their own feathers, that's not normal. They walk around like meat-counter chickens. They'll die from cold this winter."

"All right. We've already done what we could. Cannibalism happens. The books say so. We've done what we could. They got oats, they got a radio, for God's sake. A big yard. They're just idiot chickens."

"That's the problem," Rochelle said.

"But they're *chickens*. Chickens are like that."

"Oh, no. Somewhere along the line, we've done this to chickens."

"All right. All right. Some chickens don't work out as chickens. There's a fact. As for *these* chickens, if you can't stand these chickens, all right, we do them in. There. That's what they're for. All right? Now is the same as later. Simple. We solve the problem before winter does it. We assist. That's okay with me."

"We slaughter the chickens."

"Sure. We do them in. Their time has come. There. You got other problems?"

"Not really."

"You're damn easy to please, Rochelle. That's your problem."

Joe said the idea was, make it simple, lessen the bloodletting. The idea was, tie the chickens' feet to the washline, a twist around the feet, a twist around the line.

She held the chickens by the head. She pulled the necks out

straight, and Joe cut the throats, straight through, and tossed the heads in a bucket. The bodies lurched; the wings gave a slight, momentary response and then fell open.

"Compared to that ordeal last time," Joe said, "this makes sense."

Rochelle said, "Absolutely." She pushed the chickens one by one farther down the washline.

When it was over, Rochelle sat on the back porch while water heated on the stove. She rubbed her shoulders.

"That's the worst," Joe said. He washed his hands at the hose and then sprayed the grass hard.

They scalded and plucked three of the hens, and Rochelle took them inside, to start the work there.

She picked the sharpest knife and began with the feet, cutting them off, then scraping the dry yellow skin from the joint. She pulled out the last, the missed feathers, the ones under the wings. She cut a semicircle in the abdomen, out of which she could pull the interior, all of it, all together.

She rinsed the hollowed body cavity. She cut and sorted. She threw things out. Joe brought in more chickens and the counters filled up.

"I need a bigger bowl," she said.

Joe found a big ceramic bowl, the fancy blue one his sister had brought from Mexico.

"This is probably what it's made for," Rochelle said, "but they don't like to say so. I bet they didn't say so."

"Five more," Joe said. "Then that's it. You doing okay?" He was already out the door.

"I'm doing fine," she said. "I've got no problem with chicken slaughter."

.   .   .

"I should let Randolph cool down a little," Smiley said. She set her beer can on the porch railing. "Me, too, of course. How about if I help out here for a while? You got another sharp knife?"

"Knives for all occasions," Joe said.

Inside, with the sun to the west, the kitchen seemed dark, and Rochelle turned on the ceiling light.

"This won't take long," Smiley said. She twisted her hands like a surgeon scrubbing. "I'll start here and draw them out. Rochelle, you do legs and wings. Joey, you do the back and split the breasts. Got a cleaver? The virtues of time management, look at this. Assembly line, disassembling."

They stood on three sides of the island and went to work, cutting, passing the chickens one to the other, while Smiley talked through the crisis at hand: Randolph, Wyoming, and the Chevette.

By the time the chicken meat was packed in the freezer and the island was wiped off, both kitchen windows had gone black, and even on the front porch, dark had erased the color from the petunias and the color from the bricks of the house.

Joe handed Smiley a beer to go. "Many thanks," he said.

Rochelle dried her hands and waved the towel.

"Don't miss the news tonight," Smiley called. "You might see me in that campaign."

"You want a ride?" Joe asked her.

"I'll walk. Never mind."

"How about if I walk you home?" he said. "Maybe I'll see that boy of yours. Do you mind some company?"

Smiley turned around. "A concerned citizen, I can see that. Of course I don't mind. I need all the help I can get."

"No problem, Rochelle?" Joe called back.

"None at all," she said.

She watched them walk out the driveway and turn onto the gravel of the road.

Rochelle made herself some toast and poured a glass of milk. She decided to read through the papers until it was time for the eleven o'clock news. She'd watch Channel 10, and during commercials, she'd switch to 4 or 7. She wouldn't miss anything. Sometimes, the stories, and the shadows of stories, assumed their own shapes and lay like giants, almost close enough to touch. If Joe stayed out all night, that would be news, too, a turn of events, connected with other events elsewhere, entwined, like the soft, continuous organs of living things, warm for a long while even out of the body, collected in bowls.

HOW SUNLIGHT FIGURES IN

Natalie rolls up her white slacks past her knees and rolls up the sleeves of her T-shirt until her shoulders jut out. With the sun hitting her like a lotion, Natalie rubs her calves and explains how it is that throughout Republican administrations, she shaves her legs.

Her legs do shine. The skin is so smooth, she must shave her legs twice a day.

"A woman does not have a choice," she tells me. She wants me to understand how it is, in the future she envisions, that a woman will have a choice, and then she may or may not shave her legs, it will be her choice.

I wish, for the sake of argument, that I didn't shave my legs. But I do. I would say it's a choice.

I shadow my eyes with my hands and look out into the weeds. Natalie, who is my aunt, tries to forget we are related. This is an important policy matter for her. She leans back in a lawn chair in my yard and looks at me through the August heat, through glints of pollen. What she sees are my eyes, the vagueness of her sister's blue eyes, set in the bone of skull—the bone overhang of the brow at midday, a blue shadow the color of my eyes. She sees the seclusion. She sees the chin of her twin brother.

"Family," she has said to me, more than once, "is a *foul* substitute for effective government. Louie," she has said, "I want you to understand. You know this is true."

My name is Louise.

Natalie wants me to understand the insufficiency of family, I believe, because I am family. How would I know her otherwise? I would never have met her, out and about. She is a traveler. She holds political office. She has thick Mediterranean hair which she braids—one braid—off to one side or the other.

It was Aunt Natalie who called me Louie instead of Louise when I was newly born and boy-faced. She trusted appearances overmuch, even then.

"Oh, sure. A shaved leg is a pointless thing, Louie. It is spite. This is a *zero*," Natalie says. "But it all adds up. There is a weight on a person, man or woman. You carry the decade, you can't help it." She kicks one leg. She straightens her shoulders and then slouches, low to match me, in the chair. "You can't shake these things. It's like air."

"I'm thinking of getting married," I tell her.

"Oh, my God. There. If this weren't now, if this weren't *these days*, would that be a thought? Well, who is it this time? Sam? What has he done now, planted a pretty tree?"

.   .   .

When Natalie visits, we sit around. We sit around outside, never inside. The backyard looks out directly into a swamp, with standing water that shows up white at the base of cattails. Beyond the water, canary grass, then velvetleaf, then a slope uphill with the dry-land weeds: Queen Anne's lace now, goldenrod to follow, with purple aster mixed in, and quack grass holding everything together. All of the mottled colors change daily, blooming and fading, until by Natalie's next visit, after the elections in November, the sky will have lowered and the hill will be a splatter of yellows, maroons, multitudinous browns, the silver fluff of blown-out seed, and we will sit in our coats in the chairs and watch it blow.

Natalie likes Sam as much as I do. He is out of place. He is out of touch. It is a subject we have explored, on her other visits, although we have never decided if, in the end, his dislocation is good or bad. We debate the issue. There are pros and cons.

For my part, I like that Sam does what he does—which is little. He works in salvage. He saves whatever can be saved from condemned buildings. It is his policy that human beings must work to do as little damage as possible. He watches every step. I like that he doesn't cut his hair—it is almost to his shoulders—but then, Natalie says, he doesn't *have* to.

Natalie thinks there is no way a human being can *not* do damage. She thinks he should not isolate himself. He should watch TV. Buy cereal. Know the name of his state representative (it is Natalie). Visit the Badlands.

It is our old debate, and we end up talking about Sam and possible Sams the way people end up talking about long novels, saying yes to every character in the book: the pharmacist, mother, father, mechanic, the worn student, the bebop baby-sitter, ax murderer, the terrorist-intellectual, the recluse—they all make sense. Such is the horror and solace of the imagination. Of long conversation with Natalie.

Sam first showed up around here two years ago, watching for woodcock. He told me that with the mowed path, woodcock would have an excellent place to land, April to June, for their breeding display. That spring we carried lawn chairs out into the field every night and watched until dark. It was a show. When Natalie visited in May, we brought her along.

Night after night, on schedule, the male woodcock—from wherever he'd been—zeroed in on the level stretch of path, landed without a flap, and put himself through his minutes of ho-hum, preliminary beeping. And then—it was always a shock—he soared off into the last light of the sky, spiraling up until he was a fleck of dark, and then farther, and then it was all purple overhead and nothing else. In another minute, just when you thought *gone*, he plummeted straight down, a calamitous free-fall, feathers whistling, careening the way other things careen out of control. But he was homing in, and at the last moment, the whistle trailing off, he appeared like a simple pitched glove, in a dullness of landing, feet first, wings shunted back, and there he was again, unremarkable on the ground, brown and mottled gray, beeping, bland, more bland than before.

"And where is the female for this display?" Natalie wanted to know.

"Camouflaged," Sam said.

"Nobody knows," I said.

Natalie draped a blanket over her arms and kept her binoculars on the woodcock as long as there was light. After that, we sat in the dark a long while and listened. It was the whole bric-a-brac racket of swampland: peeper frogs, bullfrogs, crickets—in perpetuity—some kind of squawking in the trees, low wind in alfalfa, rattling evenhandedly.

"This scares me," Natalie said. "The high drama. Reproduction. They could walk down the path, female this way, him that way, and meet, and that would work very well. Maybe for them," she said, "all this is nothing out of the ordinary. To *us* it's a spectacle. God, this scares me!"

Sam suggested she concentrate on plant life. He said that might ease her mind.

"Tell me about your house," I say to Natalie.

"That doesn't matter. You don't want to hear about houses, Louie."

"What do I want to hear about?"

"Well, what about the drought? What can you tell me about the drought?" Natalie sprawls her legs out and aims her face into the sun and shuts her eyes.

"It might be over. There's been rain. Weeds are growing—velvetleaf is booming. Beans are bad. Corn is very bad."

"Show me the velvetleaf," Natalie says. She likes to see the evidence.

"We could chop some," I say. "It's taken over."

I tell her to stay put while I get the tractor and mower, but she stands up, kicks her legs to get them going, and follows me to the barn. In the shade of the lower-barn door, and then into the dampness next to the stone foundation, it is suddenly cool. Natalie pulls her arms in and rubs her elbows as she walks. We go through the chicken room, where there are no chickens, and on into the basement, where the tractor is housed. The big sliding doors are open, and sunlight halts outside, an enormous yellow square with wavering edges.

Natalie walks ahead of me. In the shadow of the tractor tires, she picks up the PTO shaft of the flail mower. She must know there's grease on the coupling. She must know her slacks are white. But she goes ahead, jams the parts together. I climb on the tractor and start it up. From the implement box, I sort out the hitch pins, some cotter pins, and hand them back to her. Adjusting the three-point hitch, sometimes up, sometimes down, we get the mower attached, and Natalie climbs up beside me on the narrow steel step of the tractor, to ride along. I shift into gear, and we drive out into the blare of light.

Natalie leans back on the fender; her slacks are smudged badly. We pull around the west side of the barn, and there Natalie looks at her skinny gold watch and says, "Drive me to town, Louie. Let's see Sam first. I haven't even been through town."

When Natalie visits, it doesn't matter the season, we get around. We don't do much, but it's like a vacation abroad, even so, where you see that anything people do inside or outside a house deserves recollection, a photograph. If you weren't a foreigner, trying to blend in, you'd take some pictures. Soybean, sorghum fields, blue houses at the edge of town—they come into focus, with a blunt Moroccan sun on them. If you had a camera, you'd aim it at the tractor, head-on, and at the velvetleaf, a quarter-acre patch, with its seedpods puffed like bishops' caps—a close-up of its greenery, its spires.

We drive the tractor, nine miles per hour, down Lawrence Road the three miles to town. Natalie waves to her constituents here and there—somebody at a mailbox, somebody picking up a child's toy in a yard. When they recognize the tractor, a couple of them wave back. I keep an eye on traffic and let Natalie be the parade.

At the red light in town, Natalie hikes herself up on the fender. She rebraids her braid. The sun shines on her elbows. The sun shines on the Mobil sign. On the low sweep of the curb. It's a glittery desert sun. There is sunlight on the drinking fountain, a granite post set in the sidewalk. Water loops into sunlight out of the silver faucet.

The traffic light switches to green, Natalie grabs the fender, and two blocks on, at Sam's place, we pull up to the door of the warehouse and park in the gravel. A handwritten sign on the door says Back at 3. Since it is almost three, we sit on the steps. The sun's hitting everything—every cut of every chunk of gravel.

Sam is a punctual person. We discuss that admirable trait, and then Natalie counts the businesses that have come and gone from storefronts in recent years: The Fabric Center, Black's Jewelry, Hall's Insurance, The International Salon. Natalie has statistics on small businesses, and this town is representative. She's used it in speeches, although I believe it is not because of the numbers but because of the name—Cement City—a name that gives people a laugh standing out there, listening to her speech. At the same time, it's a name they find easy to believe and easy to picture: plain buildings, a cement plant, the short run of sidewalk downtown. Businesses come and go. Down from Sam's, The International Salon—hairstyling for men and women—opened up when Black's Jewelry closed. The shop boomed, with Marie LeCou from France, but then Sam let his hair grow, and his whole crew, too, and women began trimming their own hair with their own scissors—I do. Signs of success have faded a bit at the shop, and the parking lot is back to chunks of asphalt and dirt.

Natalie keeps in touch with turns in the economy. If things get worse, she says she'll write a letter, advising the shop employees on programs, summarizing what's available. She does her job.

Two blocks off—Natalie spots them first—Sam and three of his work crew appear at the corner. They're walking back from somewhere, maybe coffee. Sam is wearing his purple shirt. He's loping along, where the curb runs into the lots and weeds are growing back after the drought. He bends down from time to time and snaps off some stalks—it's hard to see how he makes a selection. He picks a bunch. He falls behind the crew, and they turn off at Grove Street. I can see he's got a handful of velvetleaf—the dowel-rod stalks, those hand-size leaves. He's got chicory, too. Foxtail. Something very green, a plume of green—it's probably goldenrod, just setting buds.

Natalie waves. Sam lifts the whole bunch of weeds and waves his arm up and down. He raises the other hand in the air, a stop or a wait sign, and he ducks into The International Salon, a step to open the door, a step inside. The door doesn't shut. He's out again, empty-handed, and on his way.

Natalie calls out, "Sam!"

He walks up and kisses her cheek. He takes my hand, without thinking. He just picks it up and our palms slip together and our fingers interlock. That is how easy it is with him, to say hello. There is a dark, humid complex of spaces caught in our arrangement of hands, and while the two of them go over the news, I try to trace in my mind the in-and-out boundaries of that atmosphere.

.   .   .

By the time we drive back through town and back down Lawrence Road, past my house to the lane to mow velvetleaf, it is late afternoon. The lane takes us close enough to the windows of the house for me to see where flies have gathered again in the heat, inside instead of outside, flinging themselves against the glass panes and up and down with the noise of kazoos, day and night. Sam does not like to sleep in the house until after a hard freeze, when the flies are gone.

I tell this to Natalie, who is interested, of course. She says, "Louie, it is not a comfortable world. We don't fit in."

But she looks comfortable enough, riding along. Braced against the fender, she keeps her arms free, to point things out: the dead elms; a groundhog—who knows why?—hanging to the low branch of a mulberry tree.

"Sweet thing," she says. "Notorious pest."

Natalie can think two ways at once, and I believe that's why I like her. At the same time, she has taught herself to cast a vote, this or that. In her job, she doesn't have a choice.

I motion toward the turn of path ahead and over the noise of the tractor shout, "Woodcock!" as a reminder.

"The fuss! The female hides out! A good argument against marriage!" Natalie shouts.

That's how she gathers and re-calls evidence. That's how she builds an argument. She's also trying to make me laugh. She wants it both ways.

"This is great," Natalie says, as she always says out here, pointing to the path.

She approves of the lane we are mowing to the woods—the way it winds around the swamp and back through pines—because she knows I mowed it along a deer path. And one of her arguments is that humans must stop imposing straight lines and ninety-degree angles on the surface of the planet.

It makes sense to me.

"That's why you're voted in," I tell her.

I have no quarrels with Aunt Natalie.

A clump of velvetleaf stands off to one side of the path, in a bare patch around the debris of a groundhog hole. The stalks are shoulder high. The leaves span out, hand over hand, and the seedpods rise in a crown, some doughy green and some already dried to a pinched crust. Natalie jumps down. She skims her arm like a wand through the plants, and seeds fly out, pellets tapping the layers of leaves.

"Replication," she says. "It scares the life out of me. Duplication. More of the same."

I watch her tap more pods—she's planted a thousand plants—on the loose ground. She's not getting rid of anything.

"It's a weed," I tell her. "It's not family."

"Still," Natalie says. "That's how it works. Family is idiot chance. It's dumb luck. You can't vote on it. Nobody should have to count on family. Don't count on it, Louie."

"Sam won't be family," I say. "Even if I marry him."

"You may not think so," she says, "but that's how it is. That's how it is these days."

Natalie does a stomping sort of dance in the velvetleaf.

The scent of the crushed leaves rolls in the air—a musty, baked, underbelly smell, with a wave of sweetness in it.

We mow the patch down.

Riding back, I shut the mower off. It trails along, its rubber balancing wheel dragging a green stripe down the path behind us.

"All right, *get* married," Natalie finally says. "You're a woman of your times."

She's not angry. She knows me too well—since I was born. We ride along. I do my best to explain—I mention love, and ordinary life, and how sunlight figures in. Natalie listens to everything. She shakes her head. But at one point she says, "All right, Louie, *that* makes sense," when I say how it's hard not to marry a man who carries an armload of flowering weeds to a hairdresser who no longer cuts his hair, and says, "Marie, here you are."

IF YOU'RE
SO DEAD,
WHY ARE
YOUR EYES
SO BRIGHT?

Shirley, Johnny Underwood's daughter, has smooth, unscarred skin and she wears a dark-red lipstick, which she applies in class. Is there something wrong with that? This is the CPR class I teach at night. You ought to think about taking the class. Or sign up Isaiah. It ought to be required.

I don't mind Shirley. She opens the tube and holds the cap in one hand. She twists the lipstick and makes a show of preparing her lips. She presses her lips together, rubs them, dampens them, puffs them out full, and then more slowly than necessary, without a mirror, she applies the lipstick, top lip first, then bottom, then smack together, no blotting. A woman with high hopes. She has no interest in a natural look, anybody can see that. She wants lipstick to look like lipstick. She wants one thing understood: lipstick is a manufactured product. She wants this class to see. She wants whoever looks at her to think: Shirley Underwood's lips are coated with red lipstick.

Shirley knows me well enough. She knows where I live. If I asked her to stop applying lipstick in class, she might listen. When Shirley was born, Johnny Underwood lived across the street.

I live where I live by choice. When somebody says to me, "Well, nobody *else* would live there"—although that's not true—that's when I think, that's why I live there.

There's not much a person can do on principle anymore, is there? That's probably the only thing I do.

It's an old neighborhood, the hardest kind to desert. On the second floor, I open my front window like a door, after dark, and sleep outside on the ledge. The concrete ledge extends into more than a ledge—a half balcony, trimmed with wrought-iron railings.

At the next window over, the next apartment, Raymond Tourneau and his son, Darwin, sleep outside, too. Through a mistake, I suppose, on the part of the builders, these two windows join each other, doors in a wood frame. From the street, the two windows of the two apartments meet, only the width of the wall between them. The wrought-iron grille splits the ledge down the middle.

But at night, I can reach through the railing and adjust Darwin's blanket, if he looks cold.

Is this now, or twenty years later? Darwin is still a child.

He sleeps on the mattress from his crib, with a pink blanket. A light bulb is on, above his head, lighting the ledge. I hear Raymond's voice through the railing: "When he gets to sleep, I'll turn out the light."

"Don't turn out the light," Darwin says. He sits up and looks around.

"All right," Raymond says. "Now sleep."

The boy sleeps quickly, and in a few minutes Raymond reaches up—I see his arm—and flicks off the light.

It is a dark, noisy street, and I like the smell of exhaust. The diesel, river smell of it. And the radios. The talk out of range that floats around, hums through your hair, indecipherable.

It is a rough street, and, no surprise, we are wakened by a gun firing, and it is Johnny Underwood out of the house across the street, with a rifle. I see a flame like a candle at a window. And then there is real fire, heat, an explosion, all of it ballooning into the street and up to the ledge. The house across the street flares white-hot, and the roof is gone.

Raymond says, "Jesus."

I stand up, and Raymond says, "Call the ambulance."

It is hard not to think about TV, and it makes me mad to think about TV. But the picture across the street is bright as a screen, silvery. People arrive, and Johnny Underwood is standing with his body on fire, and several people emerge from the house, their skin puffed and already charred, that is very clear.

I call.

Sharon Wilson, the newspaper columnist, speaks in a microphone at a noon-time assembly. She did the long piece for *Rolling Stone* about the chain of events. She had a photographer take a picture of Shirley Underwood, newborn.

Sharon Wilson talked to Raymond Tourneau, and that's where he said the words—anybody can read them—"My boy slept through it. He'll never know."

Sharon Wilson claims she was there, but I'm not sure where she was. Everything spread. She could have been five miles away, and ended up in it.

She made Johnny Underwood out a victim. Raymond and I

debate that. "When is a man with a gun a victim?" I say. On principle.

"When is a man allowed some self-defense?" Raymond says. "When can he say, 'Not here'?"

We go back and forth on the issue. Darwin is asleep. The light is out. I am always surprised at the way Darwin sleeps, flat on his back, with his arms outside the pink blanket, hands folded on top.

In the assembly, Sharon Wilson mentions her article, her research at the time. She mentions the word-of-mouth meeting that finally calmed everything down. She was in the gymnasium, she says, the old Calumet gymnasium, and she heard the power of voices. That is her phrase. She has an idea that violence cannot persist—she says, "It will not persist"—in the presence of certain voices. She says she has heard words, ordinary human words, alter the body chemistry and placate the spirit. She is quite an optimist.

"Raymond," I decide to say, "what if Darwin says, 'Not here'? Is his a voice to slow bullets? To extinguish fire?"

But Darwin sleeps, his arms outside the blanket. He sleeps until just before dawn. It is probably dawn, in fact, not fear, that wakes him. Raymond would say so.

"Daddy, turn on the light," Darwin says.

"Hush. There. It's on," Raymond says. His elbow straightens; the light flicks on. "Sleep some more. It's early."

Light sprays onto the tree at the curb. The leaves move and the light moves. It falls at an angle onto the sidewalk. It arrows upward, and a moth I thought was a bird flies closer. Very close, it is a small moth. Sometimes I look at the light, and sometimes I look past it. And what I conclude is, a light bulb over a child's head is not what I like to see on a darkened street.

Raymond knows it. He's lying there, waiting.

As soon as Darwin's breathing slows, I reach through the railing and switch off the light.

"Good. That's better," Raymond says. "Now sleep."

I sleep very well. I always have.

Shirley Underwood never sleeps in class, I am thankful for that. She participates. When she puts her mouth to the mannequin, she does it right. She'll get an A.

Shirley is the only Underwood around; maybe that's why I'm glad to see her. She says, "Good evening," when she arrives. Her voice moves through modulated tones, very low. Hardly any breath escapes when she talks. Or a breath so light it moves only the air in front of her mouth. Her voice hovers around her lips.

"If you're so dead," she says to the mannequin, "why are your eyes so bright?" She takes a Kleenex out of her pocket and wipes the mannequin's mouth.

She's smart, and the way she talks, a class listens to her. She'd be a good teacher. I ought to tell her, or write a note. I ought to write a note, asking her to stop putting lipstick on in class.

I don't trust what I say out loud. My voice veers up and down. And in CPR, everything sounds like life and death. It upsets me sometimes. I'd like to hear what Raymond Tourneau has to say about Shirley. That's a definite wish I have.

Just a few words. He has a lullaby voice. The *Rolling Stone* article didn't catch it, but I know how he sounded on the ledge. He's not there now, and the truth is, I don't know where to start looking.

THE
SHIRT

The navy blue shirt is the one I want to talk about. I've looked at it for a good many years, on a man's chest, and it would satisfy me to keep looking, accumulating the least noticeable and most pointless facts, so that when I began talking about it, I'd be freer to pick out or discard from that hoard of material— maybe pinpointing the pinpoints where the shirt was basted in Manila, or recounting the numbers and sorts of washings.

Does it matter whose arms are inside the arms?

It's the work shirt of a uniform, but that doesn't mean a man on a yacht would not be comfortable in such a shirt, and pleased to own it—a solid weave, with worn cuffs and one or two loose threads on the top fold of the collar. I've counted the buttons on the shirt, seven down the front, navy blue buttons, each with four drilled holes and crisscrossed navy blue thread.

When I picture the shirt hung on the back of a chair—and I've seen it there, its shoulders hiked and squared off by the wooden back of the chair—I can picture it with the white linen trousers that men wear on the *Lisa-Marie* and the *Vel-Delana*, at Port Huron. But it's really the shirt of a uniform, and paired with matching navy blue pants, the luxury look disappears: the marina, the sun, the clear bottles of gin, one lime on the table—all of that disappears. And so I've learned to collapse this marina scene around the edge of the shirt, into the fine line that separates the shirt from the wall behind it or from the carpet. The marina, after all, fits in there.

But for a fact, I have seen only two sorts of walls behind the shirt: first, the reinforced-concrete wall of my office; and second, the papered wall, willows and footbridges on it, of the Ranchero Motel two miles east.

The man whose shirt it is is named Wilson, a middle-of-the-road name, I know it; a name so old it doesn't mean anything anymore. Over the years we have made love four times and had dinner together once.

Those facts tell nothing. Not as much as the shirt the man wears when we talk, when we sit together and do nothing.

Against regulations, he takes his breaks in my office, where we drink tea and sometimes hold on to each other's hands. His wife knows to call him there, and even when he talks on the phone to her, he touches my hand. His wrist slips forward away from the cuff of the shirt and pauses over my hand, and then presses down there.

We are not like children holding hands. More like the aged, who love without hindrance. Without the future offering up enticements. There's not much more to say on the subject of love, is there?

.   .   .

When name tags listed the full name, he wore his ID all the time, hooked onto the shirt pocket. But with the new administration, and new tags listing the last name and the initial only— Wilson, H.—he found ways to forget about wearing it. He's been cited four times; but he usually has the ID on him somewhere. On reports, he writes in the blank for comments: *faulty clip*, or *dislodged during exercise*. He prefers to be called by his first name. When somebody new comes along and yells out, "Hey, you!" he turns around, nods his head just barely, and says, "Harley, the name is Harley."

He likes the idea of work in a uniform, so that people know what his job is and he doesn't have to fool anybody. That's how honest he'd like to be.

But who hasn't seen men with closets of money, with stupefying power, who claim to be ordinary men, and who dress like ordinary men?

Harley says, no, in the end, those men cannot resist modifications, noticeable ones—brass buttons, a gold-plated pin, a slightly more flattering cut to the collar, tipped and lengthened, for better placement of the pin.

Nobody talks advancement with Harley. The morning the office is only one number off in the lottery pool, somebody asks him, if he had a million dollars what would he do? He can't say. He walks to the chair at my desk. People resume their talk.

"What I'd do," he says carefully, and he pulls at the shirtfront with his fist, "is give you the shirt off my back." I know what that means, and what it doesn't.

Since what he said could count as an offer, million or no, I believe I'll ask for the shirt someday.

I wouldn't think of it as a relic—it's a work shirt. I'd wear it. In fact, in the open air—where we have nothing to do with each other, where the sky looks flat in its blue colors and the wind does to cloth what it does to trees—I'd be happy to wear it out.

DESSERT
WITH
DORITA

Everlasting is not. Give everlasting a thought, even that doesn't last long. Everlasting is not for discourse by minds of this species, in this world or in any alien one, with alien sorts of subdivisions and think tanks. Ask around. Dorita, a good example, could talk about *now*, or *next*, but she wouldn't commit the time of dessert—strawberries and cream—to *everlasting*.

She said, I don't want you to *think* everlasting pain or everlasting peace one more time. You eat everbearing strawberries, right here, and they're *intermittent*, at the best. They freeze up. They suffer winter and quit. It's advertising. Don't you see? The name everbearing. You can see that. But cream is cream! she said, and she swung on her swivel chair, reached for the pitcher, and poured me a bowlful.

Is it half-and-half? I asked Dalton, her brother, who was blond even in his beard, always serene. And he smiled.

Across the table, James Jors brought his fist down. Good God, it is from the goat, he said. Direct from the goat.

Clotted cream, Dorita said.

She sat at the kitchen table, with her left leg, which was the stump of a leg, resting on a footstool. When she got on the subject of collapse, one of her favorite themes, she pointed at her leg. It was a simple gesture, out of habit, punctuating her thought, which was usually something like this: the last part of any process is conclusion. Always there is *the end*, she could say, with relief. She arrived at this statement on any subject: strawberries, teeth, *Dead Souls*, Coleridge, tin cans.

Dorita lived with her brother and with James Jors, in a house my father built in the Bouvier almond orchard. The connection to the house, through my father, was one of the reasons Dorita invited me in when I stopped to buy strawberries—all this was after the orchard died back, killed by a climate too harsh for the trees, as it turned out. And she may have asked me in because of Dalton, too—he was twenty-eight then, a boy much too quiet to suit her. She sought out company for him. She wanted him to socialize and learn how to give a tour.

She talked one night about the catalpa worms, for instance, and how little damage they were doing that year, thanks to the white larvae of some sort of wasp, which attached to the worms' backs, and fed off them. Dorita said, Dalton, you take her out to see the catalpas. Look at all the leaves.

That's what we did.

It was night, but the mercury light at the barn lit up the whole yard and shone on the catalpa leaves, silvery, huge as hands. Dalton and I looked around, under each of the trees. We found a few striped worms, shriveled on the ground, the larvae like rice still on them. Dalton, in his gentleness, lifted his feet and tried not to step on the white larvae—it was them, not the worms, I am very sure, he took so much care to avoid.

Back at the house, Dorita said, A pretty sight, isn't it? Not what you'd expect.

Dorita expected the worst. She counted on it. She probably expected to wake any day and find the leaves melted, seared from the trees, or to find the ground itself overthrown, in small particles.

It was years ago, and for no good reason, that my father moved to Florida. After building the Bouvier house, with its glass wall on the side of the orchard, its almond-shaped windows on the second level, he decided he'd tried hard enough to keep houses on the side of nature.

I am losing out to boxes, he said. And it's cold here.

I hate to think of him in a double-box condominium in Florida, but that's where he is. When I said to him once, he could build a beautiful house down there somewhere, he could afford it, his reply was no, he didn't want to build anything else. Too much space had been given over to boxes. And he wasn't sure anymore if a stretch of beach was more violated by a box or by a roof line in the shape of a shell.

I am for sleeping, he said, in whatever we have. Nothing new.

He's the kind of man who could pack up a few belongings in a bandanna, and turn himself into a tramp.

When he calls me every two weeks and asks me what I'm

doing, I'm relieved to hear his voice, to know he has got to a phone.

Dorita didn't need help, but she got it from Dalton and James Jors. She never played for sympathy with her leg, got around easily with an aluminum crutch, and worked in the orchard, even on ladders, my father told me, when there was an orchard.

It's a leg half leg, half stalk, she said.

Dorita could tolerate excess in talk; she indulged herself in it. One time she explained in detail to me how deformity was a *ripple*—to catch the eye and display a more general nature, such as the stillness of water. Water, unmoving, she said, is already, really, *outdated*.

Dorita could easily cheat with words; it was just something she did. She made up word games based on chance first, meaning second. That's how she put it. James Jors loved her board games, and adapted a Masonite square for the purposes of whatever game Dorita thought up. After dessert, we often tried these out, to see if they worked the way she imagined.

In one of the best I remember, you rolled the dice and spiraled a marker around the board until out of a series of words on the landings, you heard a chance, recognizable sentence. The game was open to dispute, of course; that was part of it.

Dorita had a ball. She wasn't well, but she sat with her half leg propped out to the side, her hair pulled up in a knot on the top of her head. James Jors, just to her right, rolled the dice for her on the kitchen table.

Soft — Any — Trade(s) — Tick(s) — Climb(s) — Green(s)

She called out, Ticks Climb Greens! Lord, she said, Any Trade Ticks, how did we miss that?

James Jors and I objected, to Greens, I think. But she argued that if we acknowledged the odds of averting solar cataclysm, billions to one, then here on the doomed earth-to-be-charred, we had to take Ticks Climb Greens as a sentence that could have appeared on a page in a book, or crossed human lips.

Ticks climb shirts, she said. Ticks climb everything.

Dalton said, She cuts them in half, over the sink.

Remember, James Jors said, the problem is Greens. Not Ticks.

Well, luckily, Dorita said, there are two possibilities here, which helps. It improves the chances. Greens as in pine tree greens, and greens as in golf. Take your pick.

It didn't take long until we conceded.

Dorita hadn't determined a good way to score the game, so we played until Dalton got tired, and then we quit. But Dorita, by any calculation, would have won. We all said so.

I have been reading—why not? Dorita left me her books.

It seems that one day there will be a flaring of light and such heat that whatever rock and vapor remain, in the place of shores and shore grasses, they will hiss and be scattered throughout the universe. Small stuff. Back in the mix.

Nothing we know will be itself.

And if there is some other planet half blossom, half rock, millions of light-years across the way, that will be lost eventually in its space, too, no one the wiser.

Or if they are wiser there, it could only be with the wisdom of disappearances, the knowledge of beauty's half-life, then and there, nothing more. And how would they carry that knowledge around, and what sorts of houses would they build because of it, and what would they say to each other, daily?

Or put on their pieces of paper, that's what I want to know, if there were paper, one of the most combustible places for words—as good as air, though. Just as good as air.

I have written all this, on paper. Here it is. I know how long it will last.

As I have said to Dalton, Dorita may be dead now, but I am the same as I was.

I don't use the word *everlasting*. I get along without it. In fact, when my father calls and asks what I'm doing, what I say is—not much, dessert with Dorita, you remember her, with the arm half arm, half hibiscus.

WHERE
I'D QUIT

The bridge on Beck Road, over the Eight Mile Drain—we called it Eight Mile, just dropped the Drain and forgot it, since the water flowed like a stream all year—that bridge was as good a place to meet somebody as a bank lobby. It was more central. And meeting Mrs. Milan there was no accident; I knew her work schedule. She passed my machine shop and even stopped in if her husband happened to be there, for a job on his tractor or whatever. I knew that on her way home on Friday, whenever the weather was good, she stopped at the Eight Mile and took off her shoes and climbed down the gully to stand with her feet in the water. She never stayed long—hardly long enough to think about being there—but she could be relied on to take that break, and it was easy enough one Friday afternoon to take it with her.

Mrs. Milan was driving her husband's Audi. She was parking

on the shoulder just as I happened on the scene, approaching from the west, and I could pull up, lean out, and ask her, "You got a problem there, Mrs. Milan?"

She was out of the car and already had one shoe off. She recognized me, of course, and waved a hand. "Gordie. No, it's fine. I'm walking around." She had a simple voice, very calm.

She waved me off, took the other shoe in the other hand, and turned down around the bridge abutment, out of sight. Most of the time Mrs. Milan wore jeans, but that day she was wearing a white shirt and a long, narrow black skirt—what a person might wear to drive an Audi, if she wasn't used to it.

I yelled out, "Wait for me!"

Where the land is flat in all directions, the only relief lies in gullies. Where the land is flat, ambush doesn't work. It's hard to die young.

So you walk to the gully. You look down in there and the amazement to the eye matches what you notice in mountain places, where your eye muscles pull at the eyeball, this way and that, to keep the various distances in focus. In the gullies and streambeds, anything like that's the attraction. Frogs jump in there like divers off a high bank, and you notice their form, the long time it takes for the splash and the disappearance of their feet. If a heron shows up in the gully, compared to everything else she's a skyscraper.

After looking down from the streambank, and then looking back again at the fields, it's possible to see that the ground is not quite level: a rise of about a foot in the beanfield looks like a hill, a place you could climb—if you could get to it—and see a little farther than you'd seen before. The plants stick up there, more feathered in their foliage, spread out, and what you think of is the top of a tree. Only the birds can take advantage.

Around here, a human being looks like a wild animal, walking upright. It's a startled thing—thighs exposed, both arms swung out for balance, the head up there reeling.

The only way to talk about her is to talk around her. If I'd paint, I'd just paint around her—the blue in there first, then the brown or green-brown, thick or watery, or both—and then I'd quit. People would say, Well, finish up. But that's how I'd paint, and that's where I'd quit.

Some of this is simple to tell: after a while, Mrs. Milan and I were a team. We didn't talk much about it. I think we appreciated all the confusion, and the lack of romantic scenery. Nothing worked very well for us; there was mud, and no picnics.

We walked the Eight Mile. We drove around. When there was a bed, we changed our plans and made love. We skipped the pizza, we skipped the drive through town. It wasn't a choice. What choice did we have? We wanted to see each other to believe—I'm sure that was it. Not so much to believe in each other as to believe in everything else. When we got to our bodies, no matter how many times, the flesh of them, the scattered patches of hair—well, it wasn't a choice. We weren't particular at all, either of us, about caresses and slow-motion rolling around. We went at it, any way at all, and kept going.

But most of the time we met on the shoulder of Beck Road and climbed down the gully and watched the herons eat the frogs we were feeding bugs.

.   .   .

When it rains, water collects in the fields first, until the drainage tiles carry it away. This tiling, often plastic tiling, opens out into the Eight Mile, and with all the water dumping in, the gully roars with it and the edges cave in somewhat. This is a sight to see. My brother in Saginaw drives out when the weather is bad, just to see the flood.

The fields of water, like pocky mirrors, go on and on, with some stubble maybe, or a few leaves, depending on the season. There'll be ducks out there, or maybe Mr. Milan in hip boots, looking up close at the damage he wouldn't have to wade into to see. But he walks out there and then comes back and steps up onto the paved road.

From the bridge on Beck Road, my brother and I check out the swirl of mud down below—the worst we've seen was up to within a foot of the top. Looking down there, if you don't watch it, you forget the scale of things, and the Eight Mile looks like the Mississippi, rampaging, no place for frogs or water spiders anymore. They drown, or wash east to the next county, and on into Lake Huron, and that doesn't suit them. The water twists around and churns up bean leaves, other debris—lettuce leaves, some kind of yellow cloth. Once I saw a pumpkin floating along—maybe it was chewed out somehow. And the noise of it all, when you lean over, is the solid noise of rapids.

Always my brother has a calculator with him, and he figures up the number of gallons going under us every minute, and he calculates, by throwing in a piece of paper, maybe a crumpled-up credit card receipt, and timing its travel from one point to another, approximately how fast the Eight Mile is moving. If he has these numbers, it's easier for him to agree to stay on the bridge with me until it's almost too dark to see.

· · ·

In the machine shop, every chance he got, Mr. Milan talked. He complained about farming in flatlands, and advised against it. "I do a hell of a lot better in Las Vegas," he said. "I win a few."

He brought his machinery over to work on it, and I liked when he talked about Las Vegas, his dream town. He said it was a wonderful city—some farmer's idea—lighting up a couple of blocks in the middle of a desert, with hotels like safe houses, where the weather couldn't foul up your life.

He took a vacation there every year, and he came back with money.

"You've heard about guys at the tables, ordering their champagne at six a.m. and not knowing day from night. That's me," he said. "And if you go outside, hell, it's low low humidity. You only need half your lungs and half the cells of your bloodstream."

We welded steel supports onto his field cultivator. I wasn't sure if his tractor could pull the weights we were dealing with, but Mr. Milan said if the thing was too heavy, we'd punch holes in the steel and that would be that.

"I've seen worse problems," he said. "Getting a tractor out of the mud without mats. Thirteen inches of rain in two days. That goddamned cat at the top of the pine tree, the very top—we had to call him Star! That kid run into the ditch and not dead. Girls kidnapped in Kansas! The Sudan. Hell," he said, "it's better in Las Vegas, where the worst that can happen is some stranger guns you down, probably by mistake, and strips off your ID, your cards, so that nobody knows where to send the body, and it's all over."

·   ·   ·

Mrs. Milan, on the other hand, was a flimsy talker, and she kissed, I think, to make up for it. She didn't just kiss me. She kissed her arm when the sun came out. She kissed my shoulder, through the shirt, at the end of a sentence, say; or in the middle. She kissed her husband every time she found him in the shop, the way anybody else would inquire, what's new. I bet, when she was alone, she kissed leaves.

It wasn't an odd thing with her—more like a gesture of the hand, the kind of touch that means something too simple to say.

However, it's also true she had the ability to make of kisses whole conversations—long stretches, with interesting beginnings, and middles full of detail and digressions, and drawn-out conclusions.

I'd look up after a kiss, to that wedge of blue sky at the top of the gully, and think, damn, I should go to Las Vegas, I'm a lucky son of a bitch.

A couple of months ago, Mrs. Milan made her stop at the Eight Mile around noon. I wasn't there. She walked partway down, hung on to a swamp willow near the water, and sat to watch. I have no trouble picturing all this. Her shoes were beside her, and she rolled up her jeans and put her feet down into the water—nothing out of the ordinary. Still, I'm sorry I wasn't there.

When I saw her up at the road, just a bit after, she was pulling on her shoes. Her jeans were rolled up.

She talked to me and her voice was the same as always, but she leaned toward me and she told me the water was swift down there. She said, "The water is swift." She told me that when she sat on the bank, the water took her legs like a lover. "His body relinquished to the elements," she said.

"His body relinquished to the elements," she said again, very plainly.

"Are you all right?" I asked her. There wasn't much else I could say.

"Yes. I'm fine," she said.

I try to think that's true. I drive over the Eight Mile Bridge and wave—what choice do I have? She's down there, the same as when I was with her. She's down there every day, talking to water, throwing away kisses.

Mrs. Milan looks just like the person she was. And the more I think about it, the more I think maybe she is.

MARIMBA, WHO WALKED BETWEEN THE RANCH AND THE DINER

What Marimba didn't know about fields and streams, nobody knew.

Not the hatter, and there was a hatter. Not the cowpoke, either. Not cousin, not cataloguer. Everything that was hidden from Marimba, hell, it was hidden. And what rankles more than that? the hatter wanted to know. On the open range. In a country that kicks ass.

On a bench outside the diner, the hatter sat with Marimba, and talked hats.

The Stetson was inspired, he explained, by the cotyledon.

"The cotyledon?" she said.

"Think of it," he said, "at the moment of cracking open,"

and he gestured with his hands. "When the hood of the plant emerges. A hat that draws the lines of the future. Dramatic," he said, "as a pot on the top of the head."

He put his fingers together, upright, at the sides of his head. "A Stetson is promise unfolding," he said, "—into flower."

He looked at Marimba and saw her lips press shut in a line. He noticed her eyes on the cowpoke across the street.

"There is no *flower*, of course," the hatter said quickly. "It's a business. But there is the *hat*."

Marimba pulled a dark hair off her shirt. "Where do they soak these cotyledons?"

"Oh, you are not tolerant of the poetical?" the hatter said. "All right, we *form* them, of course. There are factories, felters. There is the multinational hat industry."

Marimba lifted her arms and bent forward off the bench, her skin lit, and more lit, in the glare; and her body, uncomposed, somehow stood up and held. She was off in the general direction of the cowpoke, the shade on that side of the street.

The curse of Marimba's life, or its charm, was this cumbersome lurching and, in the lurch, her involuntary mumbling: *leave it alone*. When the mysteries of business, and venture financing in particular, loomed large, large as Real Estate in caps, Marimba symptomatically mumbled.

The hatter heard the noise. It reminded him of his mother. He couldn't help it. He thought he had better keep up, and keep talking.

But the cowpoke across the street, seeing the gravel Marimba kicked, leaned back, and prepared to say, "You said it." They understood one another.

They'd come to this easy agreement, after he got himself into a game where somebody said that what you don't know is the one bullet in the chamber. The one that explodes if you get lucky and it clicks just for you.

A Stetson doesn't do much for framing most faces, the hatter was willing to concede. He was honest about it, although it troubled him, and cut by the billions into his profits.

Before falling into dream, now and then, he said, he mustered photo campaigns: Stetsons on Portuguese. Tahitians. Finns. Stetsons on Lapps. Greeks. Poles. Mozambicans. Malaysians. Moslems. Hindus, too. The Japanese, novelty buyers, they'd wear them, as a lark. Like a fez.

Well, it was a joke that didn't wear out, the pictures of hats on heads. As clear as if there were hats on heads.

The hatter had a Midwest connection, which he tried to put into family terms for Marimba, thinking that's usually how it was done.

The hatter explained how his mother, in Grand Rapids, stood at a turning point, trying to decide between her husband and a professor of paleontology. But according to his mother's lists, both men possessed unusual, exemplary qualities. And both lists kept growing. She was not a moribund woman. The hatter took satisfaction in that, and he liked to describe his mother in those words to female friends: my mother is not a moribund woman.

His mother denounced him often enough, dismissed him as a big shot, but when he came home to visit, he said, she talked to him like a stranger, her kindest talk. They were not locked in struggle.

If anyone asked, the hatter's mother claimed she was not, in fact, his mother.

She claimed she knew what mothering meant, to the commonplace ear: mother the monster, from before birth and through birth and after birth; the mishmash of psychological trauma, the warfaring mother, tooth and vagina and claw.

His mother? "Perhaps," she would say, "that is somebody else. Somebody he needs.

"I fed you at first, I don't deny it. Later we just talked. Like we do now."

"What else is there to do?" the hatter said he said. "A guy can't go to bed with his mother."

Then he said his mother could laugh, with the forward-bending body, the applause, she reserved for smart-mouthed strangers.

Where the hatter met Marimba was: on the outskirts. There was the hitching post, in concrete. Dust that built up red in the folds of her skin.

Marimba had a job. She had a place to live. And she had an idea that had set her adrift, and the idea was: the universe was not created for human beings. It was a simple idea and she carried it around in her head. It made her surly, and it gave her peace.

But, in the end, everything that the hatter wanted and said yes to, she had to say no to—oh, Lord, no.

In the Midwest and in California as well, her name was Marimba. In Texas, nobody would have known it. But only because the clerk at the motor vehicle office, whose face was long and incredibly symmetrical, wrote in the blank on the temporary license: *Mary Barr*—which led Marimba to think of Malabar, the mysterious name of a place she had never seen, or was it a stage name?—from a musical meant to be happening somewhere she could not have traveled.

She let *Mary Barr* stand, stupid and dead to the ear as it was on paper. In her own brain, good Lord, Mary Barr could sing, and sun!

With the plain name in Texas, Marimba felt at ease—exotic yet simplehearted—whenever she took out her ID. The license was weightless, a flimsy thing like the one she carried when she was sixteen. She kept it folded in her back pocket, and when she ordered a drink, she unfolded it for the waiter to check, even if he didn't ask. It lay on the table as if there were no past behind it, and for Mary Barr, that was true: the weight and clamor of Midwest economics—the Jet-Dry factory, for instance, juxtaposed to a pasture; the chest pressure of morning fogs—those didn't follow her into Texas, or hover.

In Texas, she sat in the diner, and the sun angled through a screen door. Outside, the wind might latch onto shirttails, but the gusts were completely without the surprise and prolonged overthrow of the Santa Anas, the ones that sweep through rooms, damaging chrome and alloy window frames, scarring the cornea, the simplicity of the eye.

In Texas, Marimba could look around. The sun hit the floor in a parallelogram.

She blinked, and she felt the pupil and iris make their precision adjustments to the light.

When the beer and the burger were set on the table, the glass mug and the white plate were as clear to her as if they'd been artifacts on display in an archaeological museum, with neat and informative labels typeset on cards: the date, the place, the human use.

Marimba ate her lunch, like a thief gulping the goods.

Marimba herself had no particular connection with the same-name musical instrument. Except that she was percussive maybe, fine-toned. And a fluke, too, like the zappy marimba bands—Kehoe, and Jacaranda in the Poconos. And the costumed girl marimba bands—Ginger & Cousins, Trina and the Brigade—who made the rounds of Eastern Shore fairs, with their burlap sacks of marimba mallets: dozens of hard-headed hammer mallets and puff-headed mallets hand-wrapped with felt, for the crush—that cushy collapse—of vibration in wood. What is there to a marimba, after all, but an earth sound mucked up in crowd-pleasing runs—over eight, twelve, twenty-four rosewood keys?

Marimba grew up without any musical—or for that matter, any familial—heritage. Entertainments being what they are, coast to coast, that's possible. She remembered, though, the girl marimba bands, who for very small money packed the tents and the high school auditoriums for a decade, about the same time that Elvis sank to his knees and pleaded into the gray bulb of a microphone.

Right here, the only way to begin is the way you begin at a party—or in an office, or in a field, in a country you know or don't know—when you come across a woman eating a piece of food and drinking a drink.

There she is. She's eating the burger, drinking the beer.

Unless you are abducted and dropped blindfolded into a place, you usually know where you are. It's clear this is Texas. The outskirts of a town. There's the hitching post, in concrete. Dust that builds up red in the folds of your skin, and yes, her skin, too. Sweet-tasting air.

She is dark, frazzle-haired, a large, ill-defined woman, although she doesn't look lost.

"Do you work around here?"

"At the M and O Ranch," Marimba says. "What about you?"

"No, not me. I don't live here."

"It's an auto-parts factory."

"What is?"

"The M and O Ranch," she says. "It's an auto-parts factory."

"So why do they call it a *ranch*?"

"That's exactly what I asked," Marimba says. She lifts the glass of beer. "Mr. M said, 'Dearie, Texas is *all* ranch.' But what it is"—here she lowers her voice—"is an auto-parts factory built around a patio. It's probably a joke between Mr. M and Mr. O. The ad in California said M and O Ranch. Isn't that false advertising? Don't you think it's misleading?"

She leans forward, glass in her hand, and wipes up the water ring on the table with a paper napkin. "I drove from Belle Poire, Orange County, a hundred miles to Palo Corraldo, to mail that application. I thought the postmark might help. A horsier sound. Palo Corraldo. Maybe it did help."

"You wanted a job on a ranch?"

"That's exactly what I wanted. Or work outside. But it's a job. A job got Sacagawea to Idaho. A job got me out of Belle

Poire. They pronounce it Pow-er, you know, but it's spelled p-o-i-r-e. Belle Power. Not Pwar. I believe in ordinary employment," she says, and turns her head. "What do you do?"

It's easy enough to see how it *looked*.

At the whistle announcing lunch—a piercing whistle, amplified throughout the shop from corner-mounted, Safe-T-yellow cowbell amps—Marimba shut down her machine, swept the metal shavings into the aisle, and headed toward her locker.

She took off her steel-toed shoes and yellow socks, and put on sandals. She checked the pockets of her jeans for money, her ID. And then she pushed through the metal fire doors of No. 4 shop, crossed the central courtyard, where the yuccas bloomed, had just begun to bloom, through another set of doors, into No. 2 shop and the side-door exit to the parking lot.

Outside, as the door sucked shut, Marimba paused, leaned against the building, and threw her head back. She took a long breath, with her eyes open, sorting whatever smells she could. There was gravel. Car smell, metal and exhaust. But mainly it was the desert in the air, variable with blossom and pulp and a feel more like feather than sand. She shook her head, in the face of it, and said something like, "My God," or "Mother of God," anything that hummed with *m*'s; maybe she just said, "Ummmm," and let her shoulders drop. She looked like a person who'd forgotten to bring something, from far away, something she needed now. She looked like she'd taken a blow to the stomach. She looked like she'd just said, "I quit."

But it was clear when she straightened up and walked off that her succumbing, or ease, or torment—whatever it was—was restorative; she'd returned to herself, filled up her lungs. Her breasts pointed forward. Her belly shone, as the larger fields of skin can shine under loose cloth when the weather is clear. And her feet stepped alternately, unpremeditated, carrying her thighs like urns—habitual, unceremonious. She moved from one sidewalk, across the street to the next sidewalk, and she walked on in the direction of the diner.

IN THE
DISCORRUPTION
OF FLESH

He sits on the edge of the bed and talks about the two dogs dressed in polka-dot skirts the Latter-day Saints brought along in their black car, the day they drove up with an offer, a firm offer, for eighty-five acres.

This is how he makes love. He sits with his feet on the floor. He massages his own neck. If I touch his thigh, he'll turn, hold my hand. He kisses my fingers.

He says they wanted the hills, the hole by the woods, for a lake. They had an architect, a horticulturist, big-time backers from Wheeling. And the two dogs—this is the only way to see it, he says—were the visual evidence of a commitment. The men got out of the front of the car. They were in their black suits. Like a chauffeur, one opened the rear door, and the two dogs stepped out on hind legs. Polka-dot skirts. They walked across the driveway. The men didn't have to say the words, the dogs' message was plain: This is not ordinary business. This is the work of the Lord. This is something beyond us.

He says, Nothing is beyond us.

I reach my arms around his waist and hold him against my breasts. He takes my hands. He kisses the fingers.

He says, Nobody has a right to sell for profit.

He didn't do it.

I wonder where in North America the man grew up and bought his boots.

I'd ask, but sooner or later, he'll get to it, and I'd rather have it, scrap by scrap, the way he tells it. The man has no interest in chronology. I listen to his heart when he falls asleep, thinking it might slur itself peculiarly, without a forwardness to the beat, without the one-two-three. But it's a human heart.

What I know about him is this: he owns eighty-five acres. He does not hunt. He wears boxer shorts. He has one insignificant scar on his right hand, where just about everyone has a scar. He walks as fast as I do, and looks around as much. He does not know that some people are odd and some people are not. To him, it is all the same.

Until he sleeps, he does not lie still. I have rubbed his arms, and his neck, and his legs. I have kissed the nubs of his tits and kissed his belly. I have made a study of all the skin of his body. And I have learned a great deal. But his whole skeletal structure, I would say, refuses to give itself repose. He calms himself, in embraces, but then he sits up and looks around. He touches my knee, absently.

He says, When we drank those beers in St. Augustine, the sidewalk was angled so much from the horizontal that condensation from the bottle rained on your foot.

I had forgot. He knows, by my silence, I have forgot.

He is recalling major events worldwide.

And Toulouse, goddamnit, you remember falling backwards when that flower man said look up?

I see the blue sky again, the angle of red roof.

And I think it is loss of equilibrium we are coming to love.

Yes, I remember. Now kiss me. Where is your tongue?

I had not always understood how lovemaking in the present was linked to escapades in the past, when the brain was startled and forced to admit, I am in this place. And what happens in this place is *this*.

We kiss. He pushes one foot against the other until his boots fall onto the floor.

Then he says, I must take off these socks. They're the ones you saw in that bookstore, and wouldn't buy. You're too frugal when it comes to socks, I don't understand.

So I rub his feet.

Brethren in church washed feet, he says, in the discorruption, devotion of disciples. Men took off their socks. Women took off anklets. It was plain from the start that stockings and then later, so much later, panty hose, white in the spring and smoke in the fall, would not slip easily into the ritual, would not contribute to discorruption, until much later, in autumn, some-one would wind them off, they would be smoke, and wash the feet carefully, even between the toes, and then hold the toes, still wet, to his mouth.

I hold his toes to my mouth.

And then, he says, and then, take her toes into his mouth, and the disciples would be more devout in their flesh than before.

In the morning he says, The Midwest, according to periodic tables of potlucks, is not geological but biological, a feast of flesh, the first slope into the prairie, which is Ohio, down from the chin, which is Pennsylvania, and then farther along, he says, there is Michigan, hills hardly hills, which are the breasts, that's the word on the charts, girls' breasts, extreme in their softness and in the frank exposure of water-rounded pebbles, midstream.

And so on, he says. There is the four-color board game, too, with the Great Lakes, true to their differing tints: algal, buffed Ontario; muck-slate Erie; baby-blue Huron; turquoise Tahoe Superior; and oh, Michigan, mood ring, the pink, pearl, jade, navy, hazel, chamois, chambray, lapis, dove.

I dream of him brushing my collarbone, with a fine brush, watercolors.

When I wake at noon, he's recalling the refugees Laira and Bot. The two of them, he says, one from this country, one from that, packed the simplicities of those locales—the net, the goldenrod, music, mugs, wire, the red beets, damask—and when it was dark and they were here, unpacked. How can you say the first time, to refugees, what will you have to drink? When can you mention dreams, the concerns of love? When can you ask them a favor? The brown bats in the walls of the house, climbing and singing, so shock them both that one fires a pistol. It helps. When can you say it does not help?

I sleep and wake again. It is dark. He hears I'm awake, and he tells me how they—or does he say we?—sat in the greenhouse, naked, after the plants had been thrown out, thrown over there, where they still are in weeds, heaps of gloxinia and Christmas cactus. Sawtooth leaves, purple petals, the pink trumpet-nozzle flowers, gone, what a hush, and the air under glass, with no foliage to float, erases itself and takes in the sun, hot glitter. Beaches, backyards, city rooftops—no, it is not that at all, he says. Sun falls through glass without interference. In the open, it is not like that. Wind pushes dust around, up under your arms. Light can't come into the mouth directly.

But here, he says, they smell the oil on their skin. Their teeth shine and they slide together.

I sleep until morning. He is still there.

I will admit this. I have considered it.

If he is ever dead, and no longer speaking to me, and it happens I am making love to a man who is silent, I will sit up and put my feet on the floor. I'll tell him about the foul-smelling woman, Madame Truth, in her robes, who stood on the steps of the Art Institute and twirled a stocking around like a watch fob and announced that it was a penis, and announced that she was a man. Nobody had the right to contradict her, I'll say. And nobody did.

ABOUT THE AUTHOR

Janet Kauffman is the author of *Places in the World
a Woman Could Walk* and of the novel *Collaborators*. In 1985 she received the Rosenthal Award for
Fiction from the American Academy-Institute of
Arts and Letters. She lives in Hudson, Michigan.

VINTAGE
CONTEMPORARIES

VINTAGE
CONTEMPORARIES

VINTAGE
CONTEMPORARIES

___ **California Bloodstock** by Terry McDonell	$8.95	679-72168-1
___ **The Bushwhacked Piano** by Thomas McGuane	$7.95	394-72642-1
___ **Keep the Change** by Thomas McGuane	$9.95	679-73033-8
___ **Nobody's Angel** by Thomas McGuane	$7.95	394-74738-0
___ **Something to Be Desired** by Thomas McGuane	$6.95	394-73156-5
___ **To Skin a Cat** by Thomas McGuane	$5.95	394-75521-9
___ **Bright Lights, Big City** by Jay McInerney	$5.95	394-72641-3
___ **Ransom** by Jay McInerney	$5.95	394-74118-8
___ **Story of My Life** by Jay McInerney	$6.95	679-72257-2
___ **Mama Day** by Gloria Naylor	$9.95	679-72181-9
___ **The All-Girl Football Team** by Lewis Nordan	$5.95	394-75701-7
___ **Welcome to the Arrow-Catcher Fair** by Lewis Nordan	$6.95	679-72164-9
___ **River Dogs** by Robert Olmstead	$6.95	394-74684-8
___ **Soft Water** by Robert Olmstead	$6.95	394-75752-1
___ **Family Resemblances** by Lowry Pei	$6.95	394-75528-6
___ **Sirens** by Steve Pett	$9.95	394-75712-2
___ **Clea & Zeus Divorce** by Emily Prager	$6.95	394-75591-X
___ **A Visit From the Footbinder** by Emily Prager	$6.95	394-75592-8
___ **Mohawk** by Richard Russo	$8.95	679-72577-6
___ **The Risk Pool** by Richard Russo	$8.95	679-72334-X
___ **Mile Zero** by Thomas Sanchez	$10.95	679-73260-8
___ **Rabbit Boss** by Thomas Sanchez	$8.95	679-72621-7
___ **Anywhere But Here** by Mona Simpson	$9.95	394-75559-6
___ **Carnival for the Gods** by Gladys Swan	$6.95	394-74330-X
___ **The Player** by Michael Tolkin	$7.95	679-72254-8
___ **Myra Breckinridge and Myron** by Gore Vidal	$8.95	394-75444-1
___ **All It Takes** by Patricia Volk	$8.95	679-73044-3
___ **The Car Thief** by Theodore Weesner	$6.95	394-74097-1
___ **Breaking and Entering** by Joy Williams	$6.95	394-75773-4
___ **Taking Care** by Joy Williams	$5.95	394-72912-9
___ **The Easter Parade** by Richard Yates	$8.95	679-72230-0
___ **Eleven Kinds of Loneliness** by Richard Yates	$8.95	679-72221-1
___ **Revolutionary Road** by Richard Yates	$8.95	679-72191-6

Available at your bookstore or call toll-free to order: 1-800-733-3000.
Credit cards only. Prices subject to change.